HURRICANE
HAMISH THE CALYPSO
CRICKETER

Don't miss Hurricane Hamish's next adventure:

Hurricane Hamish – The Cricket World Cup

HURRICANE HAMISH THE CALYPSO CRICKETER

Mark Jefferson

Hippo

Scholastic Children's Books
Commonwealth House, 1–19 New Oxford Street,
London WC1A 1NU, UK
a division of Scholastic Ltd
London ~ New York ~ Toronto ~ Sydney ~ Auckland
Mexico City ~ New Delhi ~ Hong Kong

First published by Scholastic Ltd, 1999

ISBN 0 590 63692 8

Quotation from *Beyond a Boundary* by C L R James
used by kind permission of the publisher, Hutchinson.

Typeset by TW Typesetting, Midsomer Norton, Somerset
Printed by Mackays of Chatham

2 4 6 8 10 9 7 5 3 1

For Emma, with love

THE CHARACTERS

The West Indies Players
Otis Campbell
Charlie Constantine
Roger Matthews
Joel James
Brian Goldman
Radwick Scorpio
Andy Alleyne
Larry King
Sherwin Padmore
Roy Amory
Frankie Genus
Fish Archibald
Hurricane Hamish

The England Players
Fitzwilliam Darcy
George Knightley
Bill Collins
Charlie Bingley
George Wickham
William Eliot
Frank Churchill
Robert Martin
Eddie Ferrers
John Willoughby
Edmund Bertram
Harry Crawford
Fred Wentworth
Henry Tilney
Smith Smith

The West Indies Selectors
Vivian Richards, *Chairman*
Curtly Ambrose
Courtney Walsh
Brian Lara, *Team Manager*

The England Selectors
Ian Botham, *Chairman*
Alec Stewart
David Gower
Mike Atherton, *Team Manager*

Other Characters

Old Father Time (FT)	*Guardian to Hurricane Hamish*
Wesley Clarke	*Police Chief, Treasure Beach, Jamaica*
Rich Vermin	*English Businessman and International Gambler*
Rough Tungsten	*Chief Cricket Reporter on The West Indies Wayfarer*
Judge Herring	*Top Judge of Jamaica*
Harry Hack	*Editor of The Caribbean Chronicle*
The Secret Correspondent	*Chief Cricket Reporter on The Caribbean Chronicle*
The Mystery Girl	*Friend of Hurricane Hamish*

Contents

He was one of those rare ones,
a fast bowler who proposed to
defeat you first of all by pace and sheer pace.

Beyond a Boundary – C L R James

Prologue

The Child in the MCC Towel

Treasure Beach, Jamaica

Hurricane Hamish seemed to have finally blown itself out. The wizened old man usually took this walk along Treasure Beach at the same time each day, and he was pleased to be out again. He had been forced to stay at home the last few days, waiting for the raging winds to pass and for the floods to disappear to the north.

Nevertheless, it had been a good excuse to stay huddled inside his little house and read some old cricket books. During those days he had relived the history of the game from his wonderful cricket library, celebrating the exploits of his great heroes – from Learie Constantine to Frank Worrell, from Garry Sobers to Brian Lara. How he loved the beautiful game.

Today it was the calm after the storm. It was noon and the sun was at its highest. He loved the warmth of the baking rays on his old leathery skin and the feel of the sand between his toes. The sand was different here at Treasure Beach from the rest of Jamaica. It was almost like volcanic ash, black in colour and soft on the feet.

The old man chewed on a matchstick and whistled a tune between his clenched teeth. He felt calm in his solitude. He loved to be here with the beach and the ocean, yet that occasional loneliness which he felt stirred in his stomach today. He sighed, for he knew little else, he had been alone in his life for so long now.

The shore was strewn with debris from the storm, but Treasure Beach had been lucky, largely sheltered from the worst of the hurricane, as it had been when the last hurricane – called Hurricane Gilbert – had struck.

He looked along the shore and right at the end of the beach he could make out the familiar battered old red hull, pulled high up on to the sand. This was his boat – the one he had used when he used to fish himself – the one he had never been able to bring himself to sell to anyone. He knew he was an emotional fool, but he would rather watch it rot with the years than have some youngster sailing around in it. He had been through too much with this boat to pass it on to someone else, had spent too much time in it, dreamed too many dreams.

He had taken the boat out every night since his father had taught him to fish all those years ago. As a child he had fished the Pedro Banks – the reefs out of Treasure Beach which were abundant with fish. The boat had been beautiful, the best kept boat in the island, and he had used it all of his working life. Then Hurricane Gilbert had come along all those years ago, and the fishing boat had broken free of its moorings and had been badly damaged in the storm.

When the storm was over, he had salvaged the battered hull and pulled it up on to the beach, where it had remained ever since. He had re-named the boat, painting the words *The Hurricane* on its side. He had never tried to repair it, never taken this particular boat out again. It was as if from that day the boat, like him, had been waiting for something.

As he approached the boat on this day, he was surprised to hear a noise from it. It was a meek sort of cry from within the hull – a mewling of something small. He wondered what it was – perhaps a trapped animal?

He approached and looked into *The Hurricane*. The noise came from a bundle laid towards the vessel's stern and the thing, the animal or what-ever it was, had been swathed in a perfect gleam-ing white towel. The towel was inscribed with gold stitching and the letters MCC.

The old man was bemused – was it a Marylebone Cricket Club towel, and, if it was, how on earth had that got here, all the way from the home of cricket in England?

He gently pulled a corner of the towel back to

see what was hidden in there. He found himself looking at the screwed-up face of a tiny child. He gasped with surprise. What was a child doing here? It was so carefully wrapped in the towel, as if deliberately placed there for him to find.

He pulled the towel away from the child very gently and cradled the tiny, naked thing in his arms. He was shocked, but he could not help smiling to himself as the child writhed around. It was a boy and he had the longest and liveliest little limbs the old man had ever seen on a baby, all gangly and kicking like crazy. The baby flailed and circled his little arms like a fast bowler.

The old man was perplexed as he held the child and gazed out across the beautiful waters. He had a strange sense of a moment of destiny and he somehow knew, at that very instant, that only his own death could part him from this child. He wrapped the child once again in the blanket and took him home.

He was reluctant to do so, but he knew that he had to contact the authorities. Later that day he walked with the child to the police station. The small building was high up on the hills above Treasure Beach and the old man found the child quite a handful as he struggled the few miles up the dirt tracks. The boy would not stop kicking and whirling his right arm about.

This was a quiet corner of the island where all

of the people knew one another, and the old man was friendly with the Treasure Beach police chief, a kindly, portly, mild-mannered man called Wesley Clarke.

As he approached the small stone office building he could only hear the noise of the radio – the familiar roar of a cricket crowd. He peered inside. Wesley was asleep in his chair with his feet on the desk, the noise of his snores competing with the live commentary of the Test match from England. The radio reception had been down for days after the storm and must have returned at last. The old man coughed and Wesley jolted awake, shaking his head, embarrassed to be caught napping.

"I could have stolen all your papers," the old man laughed.

Wesley rubbed his eyes.

"It's been a long week. The Test is going well over at The Oval. That new kid Fish Archibald is in the wickets again. Best young quickie we've had for years – since Walsh and Ambrose probably. What are you doing up here, anyway?"

"I've found something. I thought you should know."

Only then was Wesley's attention drawn to the towel which the old man carried in his arms.

"What's that?" he asked.

As if on cue, the child started to wail.

"A baby boy," the old man said. "I found him by the water. I've asked around all of Treasure Beach and nobody knows anything about him. I'm not sure what to do."

The policeman walked over and peered inside at the taut little face of the child. He was still flailing his limbs about, whirling his right arm in particular.

"Well that's a good sign at least," said Wesley. "He seems to be trying to bowl already."

The old man smiled.

"That's what I thought," he said.

Wesley read the inscription on the towel.

"MCC," he muttered. "What the...? MCC. As in the Marylebone Cricket Club? Did you find him in that?"

"Yes. It's a strange mystery. It looks like the genuine article, though. From Lord's cricket ground in London."

Wesley shook his head, perplexed. He scratched his nose, wondering what to do.

"Well. I'll have to go through procedure," he said. "If no one claims him we'll put him into care, I suppose, with all the rest of the orphans."

The old man's brow furrowed. Almost pleadingly, he looked at his young friend and shifted nervously from foot to foot.

"Wesley?" he said.

"Yes?"

"If he belongs to no one else, I'd like to try and keep him."

There was a silence between the two of them. The commentator on the radio described a flowing drive for four through the covers which raced towards the gasholders at The Oval.

"What, an old Rasta like you?"

Wesley started to chuckle, but the needy look in the old man's eyes took all of his mirth away. He sighed.

"I have to follow procedure. I will have to put notices all round the island, contact the papers, put it on the radio. We'll even have to contact the MCC in England. We have to be exhaustive in such matters, explore each and every avenue. But we'll take it one step at a time. Let me make some phone calls to start with. For now I can authorize you to take him home. Leave the MCC towel with me, since he was found in it, and I'll give you a blanket to wrap him in. Let's see what happens. I'll help if I possibly can. I can see that you mean it."

The old man nodded. He unwrapped the baby and gave Wesley the towel, then swaddled him in the blanket which Wesley had found, struggling to tuck it round him as the child wriggled around vigorously. The old man stared at the child and looked up at Wesley.

"It just feels right," he said. "Like he came to me for a reason. I've always thought that boat would offer something up."

"So you found him in *The Hurricane*, did you?" Wesley asked.

"Yes. Maybe that's why I kept the old boat all these years."

Wesley looked at his old friend and saw the intensity in his face.

"I'll do what I can," said Wesley. "I'll look into it. That's all I can promise you for now."

Wesley Clarke checked out the rules on adoption. He had words with the lawyers, the social workers and the government officials. It all seemed rigidly clear. There was no way the system would let an old man like that keep a baby boy.

Some days passed, though, and there was no response to the notices Wesley had placed or the messages on island radio and in the newspapers. Nobody came forward to claim the child. The MCC had written back to say they were as puzzled by the mystery as anyone, but confirming that two towels had gone missing recently.

Wesley had gone down to see the old man each day since he found him. His friend was always carrying the kid round in his arms or feeding him milk from a bottle, or gazing lovingly at him as he slept. The old man was crazy about the child and the child seemed content and settled – they seemed meant for each other. It began to seem silly to Wesley for the child to be taken away from him.

"You know he'll have to go, don't you?" said Wesley one day. "Don't get too used to having him around."

"Oh sure," said the old man, seeming not to be able to take in the words. "All in good time."

Wesley found himself wishing, although he knew it was impossible, that the old man could keep the boy.

A few days later a miserable Wesley Clarke sat in the police station. He was expecting a social worker this morning, who was coming to take over the case of the baby. He had prepared the file on what had happened and had the MCC towel ready to hand over with the paperwork.

There was a rap on the frame of the open door. A huge, fat woman stood there, blocking all of the light from outside. She was panting from the climb to the police station. She had a determined look on her face, a harsh kind of a look. Wesley did not like her at first sight.

"Hello," said Wesley. "What can I do for you?"

"Social services. I've come for the child. The one that was found. We gather nobody has claimed him. It's time for him to be adopted into the system."

Her voice was very cold. It was as if she was just here to round the child up – like any other. She stared with contempt at the radio, irritated by the cricket commentary.

"Too many people on this island are obsessed with that game, instead of spending their time doing their jobs properly," she said.

Wesley raised an eyebrow. He was trying not to lose his temper.

"Anyway," she added, still panting. "Tell me where the child is."

Despite the hatred boiling within him, Wesley Clarke smiled his best smile – he positively beamed at the woman. Something was taking him over – an inner strength was egging him on, urging him to do something the likes of which he had never done before. His words came from somewhere within him, seemed to roll out almost of their own accord.

"No need for that, I'm pleased to say," he said.

"And how is that?" puffed the big woman.

"The parents turned up just last evening. Seems their little daughter had taken the kid out un-supervised, got all distracted and left him in the boat. They've been sick with worry. It was nice to see them back together. Moving to see a family reunited like that."

Wesley smiled his most reassuring smile.

The woman looked at him doubtfully.

"Have you got the paperwork on this?"

"I'm doing it now. Never fear. I'll send what's needed through to your department in a couple of days."

The woman stared at him, still breathing heavily.

"What a waste of my precious time!"

She scowled.

"Oh well," said Wesley. "Good news for the little baby, though."

The woman glared at him. Wesley tried to look as innocent as possible and was relieved when she made to go.

"I wish I hadn't bothered coming up here!"

The woman spat out her final words and then she turned on her heels and left, frustrated in her mission. The police chief breathed out a huge sigh of relief and mopped at his sweaty brow.

Wesley spent some days typing up reports to paper over the cracks of his lie. He created a variety of false documents.

The Lord help me if I ever get caught, he thought, as he completed the illegal file. He marked it *Top Secret* and tucked it away with the MCC towel at the back of his filing cabinet.

A few days after the confrontation with the fat woman, Wesley went to see the old man and gave him some papers.

"What are these?" the old man asked.

"The boy's nationality certificate, your adoption papers, that sort of thing," said Wesley.

"Are you serious?" asked the old man, holding the pile of documents nervously.

"Absolutely. It's all sorted – ratified by the various authorities and everything. I cleared it with the social services of course."

The old man stared at Wesley in disbelief. He was in such a state of shock, he didn't know whether to whoop for joy or to shed some tears.

"How can I thank you?" he said.

"Oh, it wasn't me," lied Wesley.

The old man looked so happy, Wesley thought that it had been the only right thing to do. Perhaps there was such a thing as destiny and perhaps the old man and the child were meant to be together.

"But still. I feel I owe you something," said the old man.

He guessed this was probably all very irregular, and he sensed that Wesley had done some things he should not have done, but he wasn't going to ask too many questions in case the police chief lost his nerve.

"Oh. I don't know," said Wesley. "Just put a ball in his hand from an early age and you never know, he might grow up a fast bowler and play for the West Indies."

The two men laughed. The old man held the flailing child a little tighter in his arms.

"And so what are you going to call him, anyway? Have you thought of a good enough name for a calypso cricketer?" asked Wesley, smiling.

"Well," said the old man. "He seemed to just fly in on the storm. Just landed softly from the sky in that rotten old boat of mine – came in on the winds, born out of the hurricane. It was like the strangest sort of miracle. So I'm going to name him after the wind which brought him here."

"How do you mean?" asked Wesley.

"I'm going to call him Hurricane. Hurricane Hamish."

Some time in the future...

1

The Two Over Trial

Treasure Beach, Jamaica

From the day that the old man had found him in the boat the child had grown at an incredible rate. By the age of three months the boy could crawl; by the age of six months he could walk; by the age of two he was trying to bowl. By the age of eight he was out every day on the beach – sometimes swimming in the beautiful water and body-surfing the Treasure Beach waves. By the time he was nine the old man had the boy helping him to repair and to strengthen the old red hull of the fishing boat *The Hurricane*, with plans to make it seaworthy again. By his tenth birthday the boy and the old man were out on the Caribbean Sea together, the old man teaching the boy everything he knew about fishing the Pedro Banks.

Usually, however, Hurricane was playing with a ball, and enjoying long games of cricket with any of his friends who happened to be around. Often he just played on his own, bowling against the hull of the red boat. The old man had allowed him to paint a set of black stumps against the hull and Hurricane spent hours sprinting across the dark sand and firing down fast deliveries at them. In his head full of dreams, he would live out imaginary epic dramas of whole Test series between the West Indies and England, in which he, Hurricane, was the saviour and hero of the West Indies cause.

The old man and Hurricane were as close as could be. They knew little else, except their lives together, and, in the twelve years since he had found Hurricane in the boat, the old man had forgotten what it was to be alone. The old man was everything to Hurricane – father, mother, older brother and best friend. Hurricane called the old man FT, because he teased him for looking like the stooped weather vane of Old Father Time on the top of the Grandstand balcony at Lord's cricket ground in England. Hurricane had seen it on TV and there were pictures of it in the old man's collection of cricket books. So FT it was, and with time, by habit, Wesley Clarke and the whole of Treasure Beach came to call the old man FT.

The boy grew up so big and so strong it was like he had a secret diet, or as if he had been born in another world where people grew faster. Yet he was just an ordinary kid, who happened to be tall. FT marvelled at his size, as did all the people of Treasure Beach. By the age of nine he had dwarfed the old man. Now, at the age of twelve, he was the tallest person in Treasure Beach – perhaps even in the whole of Jamaica. And FT was pleased to see that he was always with a ball – always he was bowling. And as he grew taller and stronger he could bowl fast – very fast.

The kids of Treasure Beach used to play games on the black sandy shore all the time. Unusually for a kid, Hurricane was never all that bothered about batting. He always wanted to bowl, to knock those timbers flying! Gradually each of the village's youngsters was going home from his or her beach games complaining and grumbling.

"What's the matter?" their concerned parents would ask.

"It's that Hurricane Hamish. He's just too fast. We can't see the ball half the time."

They would show their parents the bruises, where Hurricane had hit them on the legs and body with the ball, on the few occasions when he missed the stumps.

"At least he can't bat as well," the kids would say. "He can't bat to save his life, that Hurricane Hamish. Hardly knows how to hold the bat. None of us have ever seen him make a run."

That indeed was true. As outstanding as Hurricane was at bowling, he was useless at batting. He never cared about it. He just wanted that ball in his hand – he wanted to sling it down as fast as he could.

Gradually word of Hurricane's speed got around

the whole community. Out of curiosity, the adults came to the beach to watch him bowl – the orphan boy who rumour told had been found in a boat by the old man. Soon everybody told stories of his fast bowling feats and the name of Hurricane Hamish was on the lips of all the people of the village.

About this time, the men's team of the village needed some firepower. The captain was moaning about this one day down by the beach to Wesley and FT. He said they just had no really good quick bowlers.

"Plenty of batting, a good keeper, a couple of spinners and two decent medium-pacers. But no speed. No raw pace."

FT recommended that they gave Hurricane a chance.

"Isn't he a bit young?" the captain asked.

"If you're good enough, you're old enough," said FT sagely.

"FT's right," confirmed Wesley. "His kid's a natural."

So, soon enough, Hurricane got into the village team to play some proper games on proper pitches. Bowling barefoot, like on the sand, he was an immediate success. It did not matter where he was – in the Test matches of his daydreams, on the beach with his tiny chums, or in the proper cricket with the men – he was just TOO FAST and he was taking wickets – more and more wickets.

You could rely on Hurricane for two things – he would always take wickets and he would never ever make a run. The stories spread beyond Treasure Beach to the rest of the island of the boy who bowled in his bare feet, who was as fast as the wind, but who hardly knew how to hold a bat.

Black River v Treasure Beach, Black River Bay, Jamaica

One day there was an important local cup match, when the Treasure Beach team – Hurricane and ten adults – travelled to play against the larger nearby town called Black River. On the morning of the match, the whole team and the minibus were waiting for Hurricane as he ran to the bakery where they all met up to travel to the game. They were used to waiting for him. Hurricane Hamish was always late. The men applauded as Hurricane arrived.

"Where've you been, Hurricane? Is it necessary that you should always keep us waiting, huh?" said the captain, crossly.

"Sorry," Hurricane murmured.

"They won't delay the start of a Test match for you when you're playing for the West Indies, you know," said the captain, laughing now, and the other men joined in and cackled at the thought.

In the minibus on the way they sang songs, and, as always, the men teased Hurricane for his baby-face. They teased him, too, for the increasingly anguished look which came over his face as they got nearer and nearer to Black River. He always got nervous and agitated before games and this was the biggest game he had ever played in. He was glad when they arrived at the ground.

No one noticed that someone unexpected had turned up to watch that particular game. Leaning against a tree on the boundary was a slim, elegant figure, his face hidden beneath a maroon West Indies sun-hat and behind dark sun-glasses. Nobody recognized Charlie Constantine – captain of Jamaica and vice-captain of the West Indies.

Hurricane, rather, was noticing someone else. On the grass beside one of the sight-screens sat the prettiest girl Hurricane had ever seen. He could see that she had beautiful long dark hair. Hurricane could not keep his eyes off her as Treasure Beach were batting. Who was she? What was she doing there? He wanted to impress her.

FT was at the game as ever, wandering round the boundary. Treasure Beach were all out for 157. Hurricane, in at number 11, got another duck. As he was out bowled, FT was just passing the girl on the boundary. He nodded a greeting to her.

"My lad might just as well try left-handed for a change," he joked. "He never makes a run."

The girl smiled at FT's quip as the old man continued on round the cricket field.

That day Hurricane bowled like a dream. As

ever, he bowled without boots, running in bare-foot, with natural and graceful agility. It was the way he had learnt on the beach and something he couldn't change now he played on grass. He needed to feel the ground on the soles of his feet to find his rhythm. He just wanted to bowl fast – nothing else mattered. Today, he had positive thoughts running through his head. "Come on, Hurricane. Be fast," he said to himself, keen to show the girl how quick he was. The wickets just seemed to tumble.

Black River were all out for 34 and Hurricane took 7 wickets for 15 runs. As the players came off the field and were congratulating Hurricane, he looked around again for the girl with the long dark hair. The mystery girl, however, had already left the ground.

Only then did Hurricane notice the slim man in dark glasses and a maroon West Indies hat, walking slowly away. The walk looked somehow familiar to Hurricane, reminding him of someone he might have seen on the television. Little did he know that it was one of his heroes. Having just seen Hurricane's extraordinary bowling perform-ance, Charlie Constantine went away with a plan on his mind.

A few days later a letter arrived at Treasure Beach for FT. The letter was from the Jamaican captain himself.

Sabina Park
Kingston

Dear Sir,
I was privileged to take some time to travel to Black River on Saturday. I saw a boy, who I was told belongs to you, bowl as quickly as I have seen a youngster bowl in all my time in cricket. I would like to invite him to a private net with myself and Fish Archibald at Sabina Park on Saturday week. Subject to your agreement and availability, and the desire of Hurricane to attend, I shall expect you at 11am on that day and very much look forward to meeting you.
Your humble servant,
Charlie Constantine
Captain, Jamaica CC

After FT had shown the letter to Hurricane, the boy became over-excited for days. It was all FT could do to calm him down, keeping him busy with lots of errands and with fishing trips and work on the boat. Yet, Hurricane was jumpy with nerves. All he could think about was bowling to Charlie Constantine, the Jamaican captain and descendant of the great Learie Constantine, and rubbing shoulders with Fish Archibald, the highest wicket-taker in the history of West Indies cricket and a particular fast-bowling hero of Hurricane's.

Someone from the papers had got on to it too.

FT chuckled as he read the report in *The Caribbean Chronicle* a few days later.

HURRICANE CALLED FOR SPECIAL TRIAL

From The Caribbean Chronicle's secret correspondent

A tall, young fast-bowling prodigy from Treasure Beach was secretly watched by the captain of Jamaica, Charlie Constantine, at the weekend. Hurricane Hamish obliged by blowing Black River away in an awesome display of sustained pace bowling. An inside source tells me young Hurricane has been called by Constantine to a private trial at Sabina Park with the captain himself and the veteran fast bowler Fish Archibald. What next for this youngster? Perhaps the Jamaica side – even the West Indies? Watch out readers, because Hurricane Hamish is a calypso cricketer in the best West Indian tradition! Good luck, Hurricane!

The boy was really causing a stir. FT had always liked the secret correspondent's articles, but were these words not a bit too hopeful? FT wondered how serious Constantine was about the child's chances of playing for the island side. The boy was young. Still, he muttered to himself: "If you're good enough, you're old enough." Only time would tell.

Sabina Park, Kingston, Jamaica

FT rarely ventured out of Treasure Beach these days, but police chief Wesley Clarke was good enough to lend him the police station Jeep to take Hurricane to the trial. It had crossed Wesley's mind that Hurricane would end up getting famous and that someone might find out about the false papers. Still, it was his secret – he couldn't burden FT by telling him about it now. So it was that FT drove Hurricane to Sabina Park in Kingston on that Saturday morning.

A steward greeted FT and Hurricane at the gate and took them through the pavilion out on to the hallowed turf. Charlie Constantine came over the outfield to greet them. He was padded-up already, waiting for Hurricane's arrival. FT had always liked the demeanour of the man. He was a gentleman and FT thought he should be captain not just of Jamaica but also of the West Indies, instead of the man who was in charge – the charmless Otis Campbell.

"Welcome, Hurricane," said Charlie.

Charlie was a cheerful man, and, as ever, a kindly smile played around his lips. He stared down at the boy's bare feet. He could see that Hurricane was shaking with nerves.

Charlie nodded to FT and shook his hand, greeting him with the respect he still accorded all of his elders.

"Sir."

"Mister Constantine," said FT and nodded and smiled in return.

Fish Archibald, looking stronger and more barrel-chested and bandy-legged than ever, came over to meet them. He, too, shook hands with Hurricane and FT. FT squeezed Hurricane's arm to wish him luck and left them to get on with the trial. He went to sit up in the pavilion, from where he would watch. The ground was deserted, opened only for Charlie to hold this special trial.

"Let's get going then," said Charlie. "I want you to warm up, Hurricane, then to come into the nets and have a bowl at me with Fish. Fish is getting on a bit – I want you to show him how to bowl fast again."

Charlie cackled. Fish Archibald smiled a wry smile – the knowing smile of a veteran who had been playing for the West Indies for twelve years – and he winked at Hurricane. Hurricane knew that the two men had both broken through to the West Indies team on a tour to England the year he had been born.

Fish Archibald's first delivery was a beauty – a nippy away-swinger on off stump which beat the outside edge of Charlie's bat.

"Not bad for an old man, eh skipper?" shouted the veteran down the pitch. Charlie smiled. He thought Fish was still the best bowler in the world.

It was time for Hurricane's first ball. He pawed the ground with his bare feet and charged in with his usual huge strides as though his life depended on it. He bent his back and really let it go. The ball was too short and Charlie Constantine stepped inside it and hooked it right out of the net over across the outfield towards the pavilion.

Hurricane's heart sank. He humbly ran after the

ball, feeling stupid. As he picked it up by the fence, he looked to FT who was sitting alone up in the pavilion seats. The old man waved to him reassuringly. Hurricane trotted back to the net, cursing himself. He did not want to blow his chances. Fish put his hand on the boy's shoulder.

"Don't worry, Hurricane," he said. "Stay loose – and don't be afraid to try to be fast."

Hurricane bowled very fast – he could always bowl fast, but his nerves made him a bit tight. The first nine deliveries he sprayed all over the place. After each ball Hurricane bowled, Fish smiled to him, encouraging the boy's confidence. Fish knew you could teach accuracy later on, but that pace was a rare and special gift. For his next and tenth delivery, Hurricane roared in again, and once more Charlie stepped inside it and pulled it out of the net towards the pavilion. Hurricane scurried off to fetch it. This was hopeless. He just wanted the ground to swallow him up.

As he walked back to the net Hurricane stared gloomily around the ground. Only then did he notice that someone was sitting up in one of the stands. He strained his eyes to try to make out who it was. He could see it was a girl, and she looked like the girl he had seen at Black River. It was that long black hair which made him recognize her.

He had bowled well that day, why not today? Just her being there seemed to encourage him.

Back at the net Hurricane gripped the ball with a renewed determination and charged in again. This time, at last, Hurricane bowled a beauty which bounced and swung and whistled past the shoulder of Charlie's bat. Fish Archibald applauded him.

"Good line, Hurricane. Good bowling."

He bowled again and this one jumped up off a full length and rapped Charlie Constantine on the knuckles. Charlie removed a glove to inspect the damage and wrung his hand in pain.

Hurricane had bowled only two overs – twelve deliveries, and only two good ones, but Charlie Constantine was walking out of the net, a fixed look on his face, flexing his fingers. He walked straight past Hurricane and, acknowledging him with a nod, went straight over to the pavilion. He walked up the steps and went and sat on the seat next to FT. Hurricane gazed up at them, as they sat together for some time, talking. Then the two men came down the pavilion steps and took a walk around the outfield, still talking all the time.

Fish smiled to the boy but Hurricane sat glumly on the grass as the men walked round and round the perimeter of the ground.

"Time for me to take a shower," said Fish Archibald. "See you, Hurricane."

He shook Hurricane by the hand. He had a grin on his face, which Hurricane could hardly under-stand after the trial had gone so badly. Hurricane said what he thought would be a last farewell to his hero and Fish walked off to the pavilion. Hurricane did not have a clue what was going on and despair descended at the horrible realization that he had probably messed up his brief chance. He looked up into the stand, but the mystery girl had gone home too. She probably thought he was rubbish.

At last the two men came over. Charlie shook Hurricane's hand and thanked him for coming. He bid a polite farewell to FT and walked back into the pavilion. FT put an arm around Hurricane.

"Time to go home," he said, and led him from the ground.

Treasure Beach, Jamaica

They had said nothing to each other on the way home. FT had driven very casually and chewed his matchstick and whistled tunes between clenched teeth. Hurricane stared out of the window, feeling a failure. Back to the fishing boat for ever now, he thought. He could not bring himself to ask questions. Was FT angry with him? Why did the old man look so relaxed after that nightmare? Why hadn't he said anything?

Not a word had passed between them. FT dropped Hurricane at the beach – the boy always went for a swim at this time. FT went to return the Jeep to Wesley Clarke at the police station.

After his swim Hurricane worked on the boat for a while, giving it another coat of new rich red paint. Then he carefully painted on the stumps in black. After all, he'd be carrying on playing here, rather than at Sabina Park. The painting at least distracted him a bit, but there was a lump in his throat and he felt like crying. All he had ever wanted to be was a cricketer and he had let go of the best chance he would ever have.

Crouching down as he painted the boat's starboard side, he did not see FT walking down the beach towards him, until the old man's shadow appeared beside him. He looked up and the old man was smiling. Hurricane could feel tears of despair welling up in his eyes.

"What did Charlie say, FT?" he managed to murmur at last.

The old man could not keep up the pretence any longer and his face cracked open into a smile.

"Those two fine deliveries told him all he needed to know about you, Hurricane. Mister Constantine said it was the most venomous bowling he had seen in years. He has no doubts about your potential. He said that you will play for Jamaica against Trinidad on Thursday. He said that you will bat where you belong at number 11 and that you will take the new ball with Fish Archibald. Congratulations, my son."

Hurricane's face split into a huge grin.

2

Selectors and Captains

Somewhere above the Caribbean Sea

Brian Charles Lara, manager of the West Indies cricket team, was feeling extremely cheerful as he looked through the window of the aeroplane and saw the island of Jamaica come into view against the beautiful, clear blue waters of the Caribbean Sea. He was flying this morning to Jamaica from his Trinidad home, because fellow selector Curtly Ambrose had been insistent on the telephone the night before.

"You've got to see this kid," Curtly had said. "Everybody is talking about him. Charlie Constantine says he reminds him of Joel Garner and me."

"Fast and too tall, you mean," said Lara, teasing the big man.

"I mean big, strong and fast, fast, fast. That's what I mean. You've got to get to Jamaica, Mister Manager," said Ambrose, laughing aloud.

"Otis Campbell told me not to bother, but if Charlie says the boy's really good, we all should be there. Fast as you? Really?"

"Only difference is that this kid is even taller than me and nobody knows how old he is. Some rumours say that he is as young as twelve years old."

"Oh yeah?" said Lara doubtfully.

Lara had known that he could not ignore the clamour. The rumours had ripped around the Caribbean about this young orphan boy, whose age nobody quite knew, who had walked straight off the beach into the Jamaican side and who could, so they said, bowl as fast as an express train.

Lara picked up *The Caribbean Chronicle*. There was a photograph of the boy. He looked so young and so baby-faced to be playing cricket at this level. Lara read the report.

JAMAICA DEBUT FOR HURRICANE HAMISH

From The Caribbean Chronicle's secret correspondent

In a huge selection sensation, Hurricane Hamish, the young fast bowler from Treasure Beach will make his début this morning for Jamaica against Trinidad. The match pitches him straight against the West Indies captain and opening batsman, Otis Campbell, who has made several negative remarks about the boy, describing him as "raw and unproven and far too young". The Jamaican captain Charlie Constantine has refused to respond. The boy's guardian, who is called FT, has merely been quoted by local Treasure Beach people as saying: "If he is good enough, he is old enough". In truth, no one knows the real age of Hurricane Hamish. It should be a fascinating contest at Sabina Park, with Hurricane expected to take the new ball with Jamaica's and West Indies' leading wicket-taker, Fish Archibald. In this last game before the English touring party arrives, all of the selectors are gathering to watch and players will be fighting hard for their Test places – including young Hurricane!

Lara put the paper down. All of the selectors would indeed be watching this match. He would be there in his capacity as manager, along with the others: Ambrose, Courtney Walsh and Chairman Vivian Richards. Otis Campbell, West Indies captain and fifth selector, would be there to form his own view, playing for Trinidad.

Lara was very interested in this kid, Hurricane Hamish. He wanted to meet him, get a feel for his character, and talk to some of the experienced players, especially Fish Archibald, about him.

Lara loved the approach to Kingston – the view of the Blue Mountains set in dramatic and exotic contrast against the white open sandy beaches. By the time the plane had landed he was very excited, and Ambrose, the six foot seven inch giant who seemed to grow with age, was there to greet him at the airport.

They chatted on the way to the ground. They all had the tour by England at the front of their minds and this game gave them the chance to look over and talk to the other players competing for places in the West Indies team. The right selection would be so important to their chances of victory in the forthcoming Test series.

Lara smiled to himself. West Indian cricket was back where it belonged, on top of the world. But he knew about the new strengths of the English batting, and he secretly wondered whether the West Indies quite had the firepower to blow them away as he would wish. They would need plenty of runs, too, and some good knocks from openers Charlie Constantine and Otis Campbell would be essential if they were going to get big totals. It would be quite a series — he could sense that already, and he was desperate to win.

Kingston, Jamaica

Hurricane Hamish was lying in the bath. His legs dangled way outside the tub, such was his absurd height, and his head rolled from side to side as he daydreamed. In his dream he was being carried off the field, having just taken his 500th Test wicket. The crowd had gone wild and he held his souvenir stump above his head and waved to the adoring thousands.

"Hurricane, you'll be late for the game," called a croaky old voice.

"Huh. What, FT?"

He sat up with a jolt and soap suds and water spilt from the bath all over the wooden floor. They were staying at a house which Charlie Constantine had arranged for them in Kingston for a few days, so that Hurricane might be relaxed for the match.

"It's 9.30. Don't be late for your big day. I just heard on the radio. Brian Lara's flown in as well. And it isn't just to watch the other fast men who are playing today. It's to watch you."

Hurricane's eyes rolled. Lara here too. He hoped he would be fast today.

He towelled himself down and dressed hurriedly in the Jamaica track-suit Charlie had sent him. His first first-class game today and all the selectors were coming to watch him. Oh boy. His hands shook as he did up the zip of his top. Lord, Lord, please make me be fast and straight today. Today of all days.

FT was reading *The West Indies Wayfarer* – not his favourite newspaper. There was a photo of Hurricane and a preview of the match.

"There's more speculation in here about how old you are from that reporter bloke Rough Tungsten," FT called from the kitchen. "He says you're too young. Says Otis Campbell thinks the same."

"No one must ever know," called out Hurricane, nervously.

"Relax. There's only you, me and Wesley Clarke who know the truth. No one would believe us anyway. Who could blame them?" the old man chuckled. "Twelve years old and six foot ten – it makes no kind of sense. Goodness only knows where you came from. Just flew in on the wind, like I always said."

"It's better if they think I'm older. Keep telling them I'm eighteen. More chance of being taken seriously," babbled Hurricane as he came in from the bathroom.

"I know, my boy. I know. My lips are sealed."

Hurricane looked at him sheepishly.

"FT?"

"What now?" said the old man, looking at his watch. "You should be at the ground."

The boy always made himself late, thought FT. Before a match he was always talking too much, working himself up, fretting.

"I need a nickname."

"What?"

"A nickname – like Whispering Death or Big Bird. It'll make me much faster."

The old man laughed.

"Prove yourself as a proper player and we'll find you a name. I have a feeling though that Hurricane Hamish will be seen by the people as enough of a nickname already. Just get out of here for now, can't you. You're going to make yourself late. I'll be at the ground to watch you, as always."

From the house Hurricane could walk to the ground. All along the way children who recognized his photo from the newspapers ran from their homes, shouting his name.

"Here he comes," the kids shouted to each other. "Here comes Hurricane Hamish!"

Hurricane towered above them all, as they all jumped to touch his arms. Soon he was being followed by a group of little kids, all five and six years old. The story about the express-train orphan plucked from obscurity to play for

Jamaica had caught the imagination of the whole island, especially the young.

"Hey Hurricane – you gonna be fast today, man?"

"Bowl like the wind, Hurricane."

"Sit that nasty Otis Campbell on his butt."

"Get yourself into the Test team, Hurricane!"

"Calypso, Hurricane. Calypso!"

Hurricane smiled at his new heroism. The kids loved him and the group grew as he reached the ground. It was hot today, with no breeze – hot, hot, hot – just how he liked it. He felt fast today, boy he felt fast. Free and fast. Hurricane daydreamed and chatted to the kids. He lost track of the time.

Jamaica v Trinidad, Sabina Park, Kingston, Jamaica

He was greeted by the members of the dressing-room with some muttering and looking at watches. He was late – Hurricane Hamish was always late. Fish Archibald, his new ball partner, was stretching his muscles against the bench in the corner, just as professional today, with ninety-five caps and over four hundred Test wickets to his name, as he had always been. He was a slower bowler now, but wiser and able to swing the ball around even on the driest of days.

He looked at Hurricane. He liked the kid. He was raw, but he was quick and fiery, and he so badly wanted to play cricket, it burnt out of his eyes. Fish Archibald liked that ambition, and he liked the fact that the West Indies were churning out young fast bowlers again.

"You're late, Hurricane," he said, pretending to be cross. "This is proper cricket now. You must be punctual."

"Sorry, Fish."

Hurricane was preoccupied though. He stared out of the window. Otis Campbell, captain of Trinidad and the West Indies, was out there tossing up with Charlie Constantine.

Win and bowl, Hurricane was thinking, as he looked out across the parched outfield. Please Charlie, win and bowl first.

Then he saw Otis Campbell flow a hand through the air, imitating the push of a bat to signal to his Trinidad dressing-room that they would take first knock. Charlie had indeed won the toss and decided that Jamaica would bowl. Fish Archibald smiled at the kid.

These days Jamaica versus Trinidad was something of a grudge game. This was largely because of the rivalry for the West Indies captaincy between the two captains of the islands. Otis Campbell's reign as West Indies skipper made the Jamaicans want to win even more. They all thought Charlie would make a better skipper. FT had especially asked Hurricane to try and get the wicket of Otis.

Charlie Constantine's team talk had some strong words for his men – to be alert and be keen since the first session could count for everything. He had some special welcoming words for Hurricane. As always when he had finished his tactical talk he said: "Enjoy your cricket, all of you."

Otis Campbell and young Radwick Scorpio came out to open. Fish Archibald bowled the first over for Jamaica from the pavilion end. Otis Campbell played the first five deliveries circumspectly, and pinched a cheeky single to mid-on off the last to keep the strike. This pleased him, as he wanted an early go at this Hurricane Hamish – to get at the youngster's confidence and smash him out of the attack and out of the match and out of the reckoning for a Test place against England. All the selectors were here too. He needed to show who was boss of the Caribbean. The cheek of Constantine, bringing children to play in first-class cricket on a hunch!

Hurricane's heart was pounding as he marked out his long run. Fish Archibald ambled over with that familiar bandy-legged walk, shining the ball for him.

"Good luck, Hurricane. Be fast. Don't be afraid to be fast."

"Thanks, Fish," said Hurricane, a slight tremble to his voice.

Hurricane charged in with those long, long

strides, his bare feet skimming across the grass. The crowd was chanting his name. The first ball was fast, but very short. Campbell pulled it from round his head. The ball went high up into the air and sailed over long leg for six. The crowd was hushed. Campbell ambled down the wicket and tapped the pitch up near Hurricane.

"Thanks for that, kid," he said. "Nice gift for me."

A rage burnt in Hurricane's chest. He could not understand why the West Indies captain would be so nasty to him. He returned to his mark. He charged in again, again it was too short, and Campbell smashed an even better shot over square leg for six more runs. Again the crowd was silenced – it was not the start of Hurricane's first-class career that the Jamaican people had hoped for. Again Campbell sauntered down towards Hurricane, tapping parts of the pitch with his bat.

"Keep bowling them there, kid," he cackled. "And I'll be happy to oblige by smashing you into the crowd all day long."

The third delivery was again too short and prompted an even better shot, over mid-wicket for six more. Nobody in the crowd was speaking now and you could have heard a pin drop in the ground. Campbell came down the pitch again and tapped the turf. He had more words for Hurricane.

"You're just my kind of bowler, child. Why don't

you spare us the blushes and get back to the beach? Go back and play with a tennis ball with your little friends."

Hurricane boiled with anger. Fish walked over to him.

"Don't worry, he's going for everything. Put even more into this one. Don't be frightened – be fast."

At the end of his run-up Hurricane looked up into the stand. It was packed but somehow he picked out a figure with long black hair. He was shocked to see that it looked like that girl again, the one at Black River and the one who had been up in the stand here when he had his trial. She was there today, in the same spot in the stand – only surrounded by others now. Who was she? Why was she always at the cricket? He felt a new strength and a new determination.

"Come on, Hurricane," shouted Fish from mid-off. "You can do it. Faster. Faster."

The pace of the fourth ball surprised even Campbell. He had hardly started his shot before it whistled past his nose and thudded into the gloves of the wicket-keeper who took it above his head. The crowd roared its appreciation.

Hurricane returned to the end of his run-up. He felt loose now, ready to give it everything. The next one was quicker and angled in at the batsman. Otis Campbell hardly saw it and the ball banged into his chest with a thud. There was a gasp from the crowd. Campbell was in real pain, but he would not let it show and he just sauntered down the pitch and tapped down the grass.

Fish walked over from his fielding position to talk to Hurricane again.

"Now pitch one up. Fast and straight."

Hurricane charged in. He gave it everything and he almost fell over in his follow-through with the effort. He saw the ball pass under the groping bat of Otis Campbell, pluck his middle stump out of the ground and send it cartwheeling towards the sight-screen. The crowd erupted. Otis Campbell turned and stared in horror at the uprooted timber before he trooped off.

The facts of Hurricane's first wicket in first-class cricket went up on the scoreboard.

O K Campbell   b H Hamish 19

Hurricane Hamish had arrived. Up in the pavilion the selectors were huddled together talking. Curtly Ambrose was fiddling with his gold pendant and explaining something about the last delivery. Viv Richards was nodding approvingly. Courtney Walsh was rubbing the bridge of his nose pensively. Brian Lara was smiling.

3

Smithy the Slogger

Lord's Cricket Ground, London, England

The England selectors – Ian Botham the Chairman, Alec Stewart, David Gower and Michael Atherton – had been deliberating all day. Botham yawned and stretched contentedly in his chair. It had been a satisfactory meeting, he thought.

Two things had been top of the agenda. How real was the West Indies pace threat these days, and, connected with this, should they pick the country's young batting sensation, Smith Smith?

Smith had scored 2,000 runs the previous season opening the batting for Lancashire. He was short and squat, built like a British bulldog. He hit the ball a long way and relished fast bowling. Some accused him of only being a big hitter, and he had been given the friendly nick-name of Smithy the Slogger. However, his recent record spoke for itself. He had come from nowhere to enter the fray. The selectors had already been criticized for not picking him last summer, but the Indians had been in England and they knew Smith was vulnerable against spin.

Under consideration now was that the West Indies would almost certainly play the Guyanese leg-spinner, Larry King, reckoned to be one of the finest exponents of that art since the great Australian bowler of yesteryear, Shane Warne. How would Smith fare against him?

Smithy the Slogger was Ian Botham's sort of a player, so game was he to take the bowlers on right from the start of his innings. He was a real entertainer and a player of genuine quality and there was a chance that he could throw the West Indian quickies off their game. This was vital since they would play with lots of pacemen and, in Fish Archibald, had probably the best around. Reports had also already reached England of a new youngster the West Indies were considering who had just taken five wickets in each innings of a game for Jamaica against Trinidad.

"They may play this Hurricane Hamish kid," concluded Botham. "So Smithy should definitely be on the tour."

They were all in agreement by now and this was the final name on the sheet. They were pleased to have the meeting over, but were satisfied they had the right men – aiming for an emphasis on quality individuals as well as a balanced squad.

The others dispersed, but Botham stayed a

while, alone with his thoughts. He wandered into the home dressing-room. There was a towel on one of the chairs and he picked it up and ran his fingers over the gold embroidery which formed the letters MCC.

He had spent a few hours in here in his time and he had strange mixed feelings about this ground. Lord's had been the scene of some of the many great moments, but also some of the horrible moments from his career, like the pair he got here in 1981 in his last game as skipper. Still, he mused, that particular series had led on to rather better things – colossal things.

He stared out across the ground. It looked so stark on a winter's day like this, with the biting wind whistling around the stands. It only really came to life when the sun shone down and the people turned it from an empty shell into a humming, buzzing amphitheatre of dreams. Botham stared across to the right and the Mound Stand over there, and then turned to the left and the Grandstand.

The weather vane of Old Father Time on the Grandstand roof was flapping back and forth in the wind. Old Father Time was stooped and was taking the bails off the stumps, as he was frozen by time to do for ever. It looked a difficult task in the violent gale as the old fellow was thrown to and fro by the gusts.

Botham was pleased. He thought they had

picked the right side and he was glad to get Smith into the touring party and felt he would make an early impact. Willoughby, Wentworth and Wickham, England's own 3 Ws, would share most of the bowling, their batting seemed strong and Churchill was arguably the best wicket-keeper in the world. He was confident Darcy would lead the side well.

He felt that the West Indies would be strong, though, and Botham wondered whether this England side could match them on their own pitches. Willoughby was very lively, but apart from him England lacked really fast bowlers and he thought his middle order might be vulnerable against the West Indies speedsters. And at this stage he had not even seen the bowling of this youngster Hurricane Hamish, who everyone in the Caribbean seemed to be talking about. One thing was for sure – it was going to be close.

Botham felt impatient looking out across the barren ground with the rain squalling around. He looked forward to a bit of sun, and he couldn't wait to see his old mate Viv Richards over in the Caribbean. He hated the anticipation – hated being in the waiting-room of life. He could not wait for the action to start. He had a strange feeling in his stomach. He realized suddenly, with its full impact, how badly he wanted to win – just like he had always felt when he was a player.

He looked over once more at Old Father Time,

stooped over the stumps and spinning crazily in the wind.

St John's, Antigua

Vivian Richards read of the England tour party in *The Caribbean Chronicle*. He was very impressed with this secret correspondent, whose judgement seemed sound, and who, above all, always seemed to be on the side of the West Indies, offering constructive criticism about the team. Nobody was in any doubt as to the strength of the English, though – his old mate Ian Botham and colleagues had picked a good team. Richards ran his eye down the article again. They were only bringing fifteen men, but they were all strong players in their own right.

ENGLAND SELECT STRONG TOURING PARTY

From The Caribbean Chronicle's secret correspondent

Ian Botham and the other selectors have named a balanced squad to tour the West Indies. Their emphasis is on batsmen who can counter the West Indies pace threat, allied with enough skill against spin, wary as they are of the abilities of Larry King. The team will be aggressively led by Fitzwilliam Darcy. Their squad lines up as follows:

Fitzwilliam Darcy, captain (Surrey)
George Knightley (Hampshire)
Bill Collins (Leicestershire)
Charlie Bingley (Northamptonshire)
George Wickham (Sussex)
Frank Churchill (Middlesex)
Eddie Ferrers (Yorkshire)
Robert Martin (Yorkshire)
John Willoughby (Surrey)
Edmund Bertram (Gloucs)
Harry Crawford (Warwickshire)
Fred Wentworth (Essex)
William Eliot (Worcestershire)
Henry Tilney (Glamorgan)
Smith Smith (Lancashire)

This will be a side which, if it plays to potential, could give the West Indies a run for their money. Smith is a brave selection and a brilliant prospect.

West Indies should not be daunted, however. This England side lacks real pace, with the exception of the tearaway Willoughby, and their middle order batting could be suspect.

West Indies will look to their three best and most experienced players to swing the series their way. They will depend on a good start at the top of the order from opening batsmen Otis Campbell and Charlie Constantine, and on early inroads into the English batting from veteran fast bowler Fish Archibald. They will also expect good pace-bowling support from Amory and Padmore plus a lot of bowling from King, and, when two spinners play, off-break bowler Frankie Genus as well. Whether captain Otis Campbell can get the best out of his men will decide the series. Trinidad's Andy Alleyne will compete during this series with England's Frank Churchill for the honour of being recognized as the world's best wicket-keeper.

There is one wild card factor: if selected, Hurricane Hamish could, and should, play a role in turning the form book on its head.

This analysis was spot on, Richards thought. What a knowledge of cricket the secret correspondent had. Richards was fairly familiar with most of the England players who would be coming – several had been before on the last tour. The only one he had not seen play was Smith Smith. He had heard a lot of praise for the young man and he was not sure that their quick bowlers Amory and Padmore were a match for him. Thank goodness they had Fish to rely on. Then there was the decision whether to throw this kid Hurricane Hamish straight into the team. He knew that was what Lara, Ambrose and Walsh wanted to do, and he was inclined to agree. Captain Otis Campbell seemed reluctant, though – but Richards was not quite sure why.

He scratched his head. It would be good to see Ian Botham again in any case.

Treasure Beach, Jamaica

FT was reading *The West Indies Wayfarer*. He was becoming increasingly annoyed with the analysis of this reporter Rough Tungsten, who seemed to think that the West Indies never had a chance against anyone. Why was he so negative about them? They were a much better side than he ever acknowledged or admitted. This article in particular surprised FT.

ENGLAND TOO STRONG

By our senior cricket reporter Rough Tungsten

It will need all of Otis Campbell's brilliance as a captain to overcome an England side which looks very powerful when they take on the West Indies in the coming five match Test series.

The main problem for the West Indies is that the Jamaicans Charlie Constantine and Fish Archibald are past their best at this level. There is even a ridiculous clamour to play the unknown and inexperienced bowler Hurricane Hamish – talk which smacks of panic, since the child is clearly not ready to compete on the world stage and...

FT put the paper down in disgust. This Rough Tungsten was an idiot. What did he know? Charlie and Fish had never let the West Indies down. As for Hurricane, well, he knew he was biased, but he felt the boy was good enough. If you're good enough, you're old enough – that was what he'd always said.

The Conch Bar, Kingston, Jamaica

A black van with blacked-out windows was parked in the street outside The Conch Bar.

Inside, a fat, ugly man sat in the corner of this dark and dingy bar in the Jamaican capital, reading the newspapers and alternately scoffing a massive ice-cream and swigging from a large bottle of beer.

Rich Vermin had both papers with him as he studied the news of the England side that day. He pored over both *The West Indies Wayfarer* and *The Caribbean Chronicle.*

He read the secret correspondent of *The Caribbean Chronicle* with much annoyance – it made him feel nervous. He knew this was right – Constantine and Archibald were two of the all-time greats. They would play an important part in the series. What was more, he was worried about this Hurricane Hamish – the young sensation.

He turned to Rough Tungsten's article with some amusement. The idiot was starting to earn his money, he thought. This was just the sort of reporting that was required. The West Indies had to be undermined at all costs.

He smiled. With the plans he had up his sleeve, the England players looked like a winning side to him. It had to be a winning side, because Rich Vermin, who was an extravagant and addicted gambler, had one million pounds riding on the result of the series. If England won he made that money — one million beautiful smackers.

He had not come all this way to the West Indies to be denied his reward and he had ways of making sure he got what he wanted. Thank goodness the selectors had picked Smithy the Slogger — now there was a batsman who would give the West Indies bowlers what for, especially with a little help. And Rich Vermin had a few ideas about what that help might be.

He laughed a full-bellied laugh and took another huge mouthful of ice-cream. The battle lines were being drawn. He was looking forward to his next meeting with Rough Tungsten and Otis Campbell.

4

The Three Villains

The offices of The West Indies Wayfarer, *Kingston, Jamaica*

Rough Tungsten, senior cricket reporter on *The West Indies Wayfarer*, sat at his desk staring into the dirty ashtray in front of him, and absent-mindedly fingered the cigarette butts. He was a small, nervous man, always a bit jumpy, constantly twitching and fiddling with something, and at the moment he was even more agitated than usual.

He felt very tired and downcast, and he looked it – with red, bloodshot eyes and the dark shadow of several days' growth of beard. It had been a long week and, whatever he had tried and whatever he had written, he could not stop the momentum surrounding this child, Hurricane Hamish.

On Rich Vermin's instructions, he had written everything he could to undermine the boy's chances of playing against England, but the people of the West Indies still wanted him in the team so much. More importantly, the selectors seemed equally convinced. The article he had just finished and sent down to the editing room was his final throw of the dice.

He knew that his fellow conspirators were not pleased or impressed by his battle of opinion with the secret correspondent on the rival paper *The Caribbean Chronicle*. The secret correspondent seemed to be much more the voice of the people than he ever did.

The phone on his desk rang and he picked it up hesitantly.

"Yeah?" Rough said.

"Is that you, Tungsten?"

Rough Tungsten recognized the voice.

"How are you, Rich?" he said, pretending to be cheerful.

"Angry," said the voice. "Angry with you in particular."

Rough winced and played more nervously with the cigarette butts.

"Where are we meeting tonight, Rich?" he asked.

"In The Conch Bar, at nine," Rich Vermin said curtly. "Bring the first editions of *The Wayfarer* with today's article of yours. Not that it will be helpful, though. I'm sure it will be as useless and pathetic as all the others. And we are not helped by the fact that you are losing the war of words to this secret correspondent at *The Caribbean Chronicle*."

There was a silence down the line. Rough could

hear Rich Vermin breathing heavily, which was always a bad sign.

"Is Otis coming?" asked Rough, trying to change the subject.

"Of course Otis is coming. If England are to win the series, we need to find some way of destroying this boy Hurricane Hamish, or whatever his stupid name is. Otis is crucial to that."

Rough Tungsten picked at the cigarette butts. He wondered if it was all worth it. Yet, he needed the money. He had some very old debts to pay off and Vermin had promised him a lot of money if he successfully helped to undermine the West Indies team.

"The boy may be too good, Rich. Has it ever occurred to you he might just be too good to leave out of the side, whatever I write?"

There was a snort down the line.

"Of course he's too good, you fool. But we'll see about that. Nobody stands in the way of Mister Richard Vermin! I've got another idea and a little job for you, Rough Tungsten. We'll discuss it later at The Conch Bar."

With that Rich Vermin hung up and the ominous dull tone of the dead line buzzed loudly from the receiver into Rough Tungsten's ear.

The Conch Bar, Kingston, Jamaica

Later that evening it was Rough who was the first of the three conspirators to arrive at the bar. He ordered a beer and sat sipping it distractedly at one of the heavy wooden tables which was tucked away into a dark corner of the room. His eyelids still felt very heavy. He was so fed up with all of this. What did Rich Vermin expect him to do? Everybody was so excited about this boy Hurricane Hamish that it did not seem to matter what Rough wrote. His words were being ignored and his reputation as a journalist was in tatters.

He was pleased to have a few moments to himself before the others arrived. He looked through *The West Indies Wayfarer* and grimaced as he read his own words. Once again, he had written an article arguing that the boy was too young. There was nothing new in that, but he had nothing else to try to criticize him with. He had seen the Jamaica game against Trinidad – it was obvious to anyone who knew anything about cricket that the boy was special and that he should be given his chance. This could be a difficult and long evening, he thought.

The old door to the bar creaked a warning and Rough became even more agitated as Rich Vermin walked into the bar. Rich was a big man and he slowly sidled over to the table where Rough was sitting. Without a word of greeting, he slapped a newspaper down on the wooden table in front of Rough.

"Now look!" said Rich Vermin.

It was the first edition of *The Caribbean*

Chronicle, with another of those articles from the secret correspondent. Rough Tungsten was sick of these.

WE WANT HURRICANE HAMISH!

From The Caribbean Chronicle's secret correspondent

The people of the West Indies have made it quite clear that they want one thing above all others from tomorrow's selection meeting to pick the side for the first Test against England at Georgetown, Guyana. They want to see the inclusion in the side of that tall youngster with no age, who comes from Treasure Beach, has only played one first-class match and who goes by the name of Hurricane Hamish. To look forward to above all else will be the confrontation between England new boy Smithy the Slogger and Hurricane…

The article went on, but Rough had read enough. He put the paper down in a pool of beer on the table and passed his hands over his face in some despair. He wondered for the millionth time who the rival newspaper's secret correspondent was. Rich Vermin just stood there glaring at him.

The bar door creaked again and Otis Campbell walked in. He looked like a cowboy, disguised in an American ten-gallon hat and dark glasses, so that nobody would recognize him as the captain of the West Indies. He looked furtively around the bar and made his way over to the table in the corner to join Rich and Rough.

"Hello gentlemen," he whispered. "We three meet again."

Rich Vermin signalled to the barman who brought them three bottles of Red Stripe.

"What's the latest on the team, Otis?" asked Rich Vermin, who had made himself red in the face with his rage.

"Hopeless. I will be a lone voice on selection. All the others – Lara, Ambrose, Walsh and now even Richards – they all want this baby-face in the team. They have made that quite clear. Indeed, if I make a fuss I could blow our cover. We just have to go with it and come up with some more and better plans later."

Rich Vermin slammed his fist down on the table in anger.

"Useless! Both of you! What do you think I pay you for! There's a lot of money riding on this!" he shouted.

Some other people in the bar looked round and Otis pulled up the collar of his jacket and slouched further down in his chair. Rough shifted around nervously in his seat.

"Sorry," said Rough, helplessly.

"I'll do my best," said Otis, with a slight sneer.

Otis hated kowtowing to this bully. He hated being in a plot to make his own team lose and being in the pay of Rich Vermin. Yet, he needed it for his dream. He had his mind set on a farm in Trinidad – to keep him comfortable when his cricket days ended. He lived alone – an isolated and unpopular man. He needed the farm to give him a business, something to work at and keep him occupied when he retired. He had to put up the money within months. Vermin's offer seemed the only way to ensure he had more than an empty life after cricket. He felt, too, that his eye for a ball was going – he'd made so few runs in the last two series. So many people seemed to want Charlie Constantine to replace him as West Indies skipper, sometimes he felt his days were already numbered.

So it was that Rich Vermin had also sucked in Otis Campbell to help with his plot. For the men to make their money, the West Indies had to lose this Test series to the England tourists. Rich Vermin would try any methods and he would stop at nothing to get the result that he wanted.

Rich was paying Rough Tungsten to try to undermine the West Indies in the press, to try to ensure they chose a weakened team and to write articles to attack the confidence of players. Rough was a well-known commentator on cricket and had been offering judgements for many years, but the problem was that recently his readers had been preferring the opinions of the secret correspondent of the rival paper.

Otis Campbell, the troubled and insecure West Indies captain, had the main job to make sure England won. After he had been bowled out twice by Hurricane Hamish when he played for Trinidad against Jamaica, Otis realized that Hurricane would be too fast and too good for the English. The only way he could let England win was to try to keep Hurricane out of the West Indies team. It was a strange and sad situation for sport – a captain trying to get his own side to lose. FT's reservations about Otis Campbell were spot on.

Rich Vermin gradually calmed down.

"Listen," he said. "Great minds always have a second plan. Especially when a million pounds is at stake."

He leant forward at the table and the three of them moved their heads together.

"I heard something the other day that may be useful," Rich said. "I may have another idea to keep this kid out of the team. It may involve you in a little investigative work, Rough."

A crooked smile came across Rich Vermin's face to replace his anger. The three villains huddled closer together.

Treasure Beach, Jamaica

The following afternoon Hurricane was swimming out in the bay at Treasure Beach. He knew that today the selectors would announce the team for the first Test against England. As he bobbed with the waves, feeling strong and free in the water and soothing and loosening his muscles for his bowling, he hoped and prayed he would be chosen. Mr Lara had spoken to him after the Jamaica versus Trinidad game and had been very encouraging. He had heard from some of the other players, though, that Otis Campbell had expressed doubts about his ability, which seemed strange since Hurricane had got him out twice in that match.

After his swim he walked back along Treasure Beach to the house. FT was sitting reading *The Caribbean Chronicle* with the radio on, the familiar beat of the reggae music filling the room. He looked up as Hurricane came in.

"Any news?" asked Hurricane.

"Not yet."

"Why are they taking so long?" said the boy, in anguish.

Hurricane paced around the room. If he was not to be picked, at least let him hear the news as soon as possible.

"Sit down, child. You shouldn't worry about these things you cannot control."

FT seemed calm, but his insides were churning as much as Hurricane's. He was only protecting the boy and trying to steady their nerves.

At that moment the music on the radio stopped and was replaced by the voice of an announcer. The news of the team was broadcast across the Caribbean.

"We interrupt this record to bring you the West Indies twelve named in the squad against England for the first Test at Georgetown, Guyana. It is as follows:

Otis Campbell, captain (Trinidad)
Charlie Constantine, vice-captain (Jamaica)
Roger Matthews (Barbados)
Joel James (Barbados)
Brian Goldman (Antigua)
Andy Alleyne, wicket-keeper (Trinidad)
Larry King (Guyana)
Sherwin Padmore (Trinidad)
Roy Amory (Antigua)
Frankie Genus (St Vincent)
Fish Archibald (Jamaica)
and..."

The announcer hesitated.

"...and new cap Hurricane Hamish from Treasure Beach, Jamaica, who is expected to play in the final eleven...

"With that exciting news, which I think we had all been hoping for, I now return you to the music..."

FT chuckled – that old, warm, familiar chuckle.

"What did I tell you?" said the old man. "If you're good enough, you're old enough."

Hurricane was staring out of the window in shock. It was going to happen, his dream would come true. Surely nothing could stop it now. The old man came over to him and reached up and put his arm around him.

"You made it, son. You came mewling and screaming and flailing your limbs in a little fishing boat and made it all the way to the West Indies team. Well done, my son."

Hurricane looked down at him. FT had tears in his eyes.

"Promise me one thing," said FT, trying to keep hold of his quivering voice.

"What?" asked Hurricane. "Anything for you, FT."

"Be fast against the English," said the old man, and he started to chuckle again. "Be fast."

Hurricane flashed that bright wicked smile of his.

"You don't have to worry about that, FT," Hurricane said. "I will be. I promise."

5

The Secret File

Treasure Beach, Jamaica

FT was in a good mood the next morning. After all, he had a trip to the Test match in Guyana to look forward to. He chewed a matchstick and whistled between his teeth as he cooked breakfast for himself and Hurricane. He turned the sizzling sardines with a fork and squeezed some lemon juice into the frying pan. As he cooked, he read the paper and revelled in the pleasure of the cricket report in *The Caribbean Chronicle*.

He had now become very loyal to *The Caribbean Chronicle* because he welcomed the words of encouragement for Hurricane from the secret correspondent, who seemed genuinely to represent the views of the people of the West Indies. As he moved the fish round the pan, FT read the article which confirmed yesterday's wonderful, life-changing news.

TEST MATCH CALL UP FOR HURRICANE HAMISH

From The Caribbean Chronicle's secret correspondent

The news the whole of the Caribbean has been waiting for broke yesterday as the lanky youngster from Treasure Beach made it to the West Indies side to play England in the first Test.

This is despite surprising stories of dissent from West Indies captain Otis Campbell, which have reached *The Caribbean Chronicle*. Campbell was against the selection of the young fast bowler but was seemingly out-voted and overruled by the other selectors. Brian Lara, so impressed by the performance Hurricane turned in for Jamaica against Trinidad, when he took 5 for 21 and 5 for 43 (taking the wicket of Campbell twice), pushed especially hard for his inclusion.

Chairman of selectors Vivian Richards vowed always to be prepared to choose young West Indian players who were good enough, and insisted that Hurricane was ready, despite being picked for his country having played only one first-class game, something which is unprecedented in recent West Indies cricket history.

FT smiled and sipped from his mug of tea. Viv Richards understood – if you're good enough, you're old enough. Hurricane would enjoy reading this when he got back from the beach. Where was the boy? Late for breakfast as usual.

He was distracted from these thoughts by a knock on the door. FT got up to open it, still smiling. He was surprised to see burly Wesley Clarke standing there, holding his policeman's cap down by his side. The officer's ashen appearance and worried frown immediately wiped the smile from FT's face.

"What is it, Wesley?" asked FT. "You look as though you just saw a ghost."

"Where's Hurricane?" Wesley asked, peering nervously past FT into the house.

"He's at the beach. Why do you ask?"

Wesley took out a blue-spotted handkerchief and mopped his brow.

"Thank goodness," he said quietly. "That's probably best for now. Something dreadful has happened."

FT told Wesley to come in and the police chief sat down heavily in a chair at the breakfast table. FT could see how upset Wesley was and did not press him to talk at first. He made the policeman some tea. Wesley just stared down at the table. His hands were shaking and he seemed beside himself with worry.

"What is it?" FT implored eventually. "What on earth has happened to upset you so much, Wesley?"

FT stared at his friend, who eventually raised his head to meet the eyes of the old man.

Wesley Clarke gulped and began his story.

"I have never been totally honest with you, old friend," he began. "About Hurricane, I mean – and about the things I did twelve years ago. They are back to haunt me now though. I thought this might happen one day."

"What things?" said FT. "What on earth do you mean?"

"I cut some corners all those years ago. I did something that I've never told anyone about. I invented some things. I told some lies. I forged some papers. I never told you because I never wanted you to have to worry that Hurricane was not safe with you. I kept it all to myself. It would all have been OK. It was the right thing to do. No one need ever have known. How was I supposed to know he would really end up being good enough to play for the West Indies? And how was I supposed to know that someone wanted to damage him – to keep him out of the team at any cost? How was I supposed to know that..."

"Hey. Slow down," said FT. "You mean I became Hurricane's guardian because you fixed it?"

"That's exactly what happened," said Wesley.

FT's mouth had fallen open. Perhaps he had half-suspected some of this over the years, but had never wanted to ask any questions. Just having Hurricane with him had always been too important.

"So what has happened all of a sudden, Wesley? Why all of this concern now? Who knows about this?"

"The whole of the Caribbean – thanks to that Tungsten fellow."

"What do you mean?" FT asked. He was still catching up with this bizarre twist of events.

Wesley gulped again and continued.

"Some things went missing from the police station yesterday, which were probably taken quite late on in the evening. Some papers were stolen, including the documentation about your finding of Hurricane and about the adoption and the certificates I sorted out. I kept a secret file.

"And then this article appears. Have you seen *The West Indies Wayfarer* today? Clearly someone has got their hands on Hurricane's file – and the MCC towel which was with it – and have passed them on to this dreadful reporter of theirs. Or maybe Tungsten pinched them himself. He's got his hands on this stuff and then gone and done some checking with the authorities. He's rumbled me."

Wesley felt sick with worry and remorse.

"I only get *The Caribbean Chronicle* now," FT said. "I've stopped reading *The Wayfarer* because I prefer to read the secret correspondent on the cricket to that Rough Tungsten chap you mention. He's so negative about Hurricane."

"Well, nothing has changed," said Wesley. "Look what the man has written this time."

FT frowned. What was Wesley talking about? Wesley handed FT the paper.

"You're not going to like it," he warned.

HURRICANE HAMISH ILLEGAL

By our senior cricket reporter Rough Tungsten

Information has reached *The West Indies Wayfarer* to show that Hurricane Hamish does not qualify to play cricket for the West Indies. The tall boy was illegally adopted only twelve years ago and his origins remain uncertain. He does not possess papers of nationality, citizenship or residency to qualify him for the West Indies team. What is more, *The West Indies Wayfarer* can reveal that the boy was found in an MCC towel – casting grave doubts on his origin and suggesting that he might actually be English. Indeed, was his guardian ever really granted any official papers to even make him a resident of our islands?

The Wayfarer is now sending reporters to England to solve this mystery. I suggest that only West Indians can play for the West Indies and that Hurricane's appearance at Georgetown in the first Test must be blocked by the law of the land.

Rough Tungsten had done the job he had been asked to do by Rich Vermin and followed the plan to the letter. Through his contacts around the island Rich had heard some rumours about the strange background of Hurricane Hamish and some stories of how an old man had found him and had come to look after the boy and raise him as his own. He suspected it would be worth pursuing and had told Rough to use his skills as a journalist to find out more.

Rough had asked around and had discovered that there was a police chief who had been involved in the adoption up at the local Treasure Beach police station. He had been up to Wesley Clarke's office the previous evening. His plan had been to distract the man into town on some false premise and sneak back and break in and rob the necessary files. He had not needed to do that.

Wesley had been sleeping like a baby, just as he had been when FT had first brought Hurricane up the hill to the police station those twelve years before. While Wesley snored away, Rough had gone through the files and stolen one with all he needed to know about Hurricane Hamish. It had some details of the finding of Hurricane and his adoption, which Wesley had helped to organize for FT. Yet there were none of the officially-stamped documents for such a case. There were no nationality papers or citizenship papers there at all with the required signatures from the authorities. It all looked highly suspect, confirmed when Rough contacted the various government departments, who had no proper records for anyone called Hurricane Hamish.

No sooner had Hurricane been picked for the West Indies, than Rough ran his story to threaten all of this.

The silence hung in the air between FT and Wesley. The only noise was the buzzing of some flies against the window. FT put the paper down.

"Oh, Wesley. What a disaster!" he said.

Wesley was wandering around the room, as if in a daze.

"I'm going to Kingston to see the chief of police for the whole of Jamaica to see what can be done," he said. "I will be stripped of my badge. I'll have to tell the truth. Everything I did.

"This whole business will require a court ruling by a judge which may take some weeks," Wesley continued. "I'll do all I can. It's impossible for Hurricane to play in the first Test, though. In fact, he may never get to play for the West Indies at this rate."

Wesley spoke very quietly. He gulped again.

"You may even lose him, FT," he said. "I feel very responsible."

Wesley was shaking. Despite the fear rising within him FT felt a surge of kindness for the man, who had risked so much and had lived with a secret so that he and Hurricane might be together.

"Oh no," said FT. "It's nobody's fault. You did what you felt was best for the boy. And for me."

"I am so sorry. I was asleep when the things were stolen. And it was me who was the dishonest one. You have done nothing to deserve this shock. One thing is for sure. Somebody is determined to keep your boy out of the West Indies side."

"And this reporter Rough Tungsten seems to want that, too," said FT.

The two men stared at the newspaper on the table.

"I'm sorry," said Wesley. "And I know how much Hurricane will be hurt."

"Oh, good grief!" said FT, in panic. "How can I tell the boy this? He's due back soon. He'll be destroyed by this news when he comes home."

The sardines started to give off a cloud of smoke. They had burnt to a frazzle in the pan.

The phone did not stop all day and FT received a lot of support. Most importantly, there was a call from Brian Lara to say that they had received a letter from a government lawyer, which indeed confirmed that Hurricane could not play against England until there had been a proper hearing in a court of law about the matter of his eligibility. He was very friendly and told FT they would do all they could to help to get Hurricane's papers sorted, but that the matter was out of their hands.

There was also a call from the island police chief. He explained that Wesley had been suspended from duties and he confirmed to FT that there would be a court hearing on the matter as soon as possible. There was no malice from him. Everybody seemed to want the boy to play, and were pulling together to try to make it happen.

Hurricane was inconsolable. When FT told him and showed him the paper, he just flopped his long body into a chair and buried his face in his hands. Soon he left the house to head back for the beach, only returning later after dark. He wandered the beach for days after this, unable to settle to anything, just sitting up on the rocks for hours staring out to sea. He thought the chance was gone for ever. He would never wear the maroon cap of the West Indies team.

A card came a few days later from Charlie Constantine and Fish Archibald. It simply said: "We look forward to playing with you soon."

Hurricane read it, and put it down on the table.

"Some chance," he said and walked straight out of the door and off to the beach.

FT simply blamed himself. He knew that it was because he had been so desperate to have the boy that, out of friendship for him, Wesley had bypassed some procedures. Now everyone was paying for it. He could hardly bear to see Hurricane so upset like this.

The Conch Bar, Kingston, Jamaica

It was a wild and windy night when the three conspirators met once again in the dingy gloom of The Conch Bar. There was a violent storm and outside the thunder clattered and the lightning flashed. Rough Tungsten was drenched when he arrived. He took their usual place in the shadows of the back corner of the bar and sat dripping at the table. The rain drummed on the metal roof of the building and through the water pounding on the window Rough could just make out the black van which was pulling up outside.

The door creaked and two figures came in together, huddled under an umbrella. One was Otis, wearing his usual disguise of dark glasses and cowboy hat, who glanced around the bar, pleased to see it was deserted. Tonight everyone else was hiding at home out of the rain.

Rough noticed that, for a change, Rich Vermin had a huge smile on his face. This made the reporter feel a little better. Rich and Otis came over and sat at the table opposite him. Rich signalled to the barman for some beers and the conspirators sat drinking in silence for some time, contemplating the events of the last few days.

"Good work, Rough," Rich said eventually.

Rough could not resist a smile.

"What next then?" said Rich. "I want you to stay one step ahead all the time – especially with that stupid secret correspondent so much on Hurricane's side."

Rough smiled.

"Never worry, Rich. Like you told me, I'll write an article about some parents from England who claim the boy. It should delay things a little. Long enough for the series to be lost before Hurricane's papers are cleared."

Rich cackled.

"You do that. Meanwhile I'll find some suitable people. A nice homely couple to say the boy is theirs. Money can buy you anything, you know."

He winked at Rough.

"I like it," said Rough. "Keep that kid out of the side and we can leave the rest to Otis, can't we, Mister West Indies skipper?"

Otis Campbell forced a grin. Not having Hurricane in the team would certainly make his job much easier. He felt strange, though, setting out to make his own team lose.

"Do you know what to do now, Otis?" said Rich, rather menacingly.

Otis had his losing tactics well thought out.

"Simple," said Otis. "I use Fish Archibald as little

as possible and I avoid bowling Larry King at their new opener, Smithy the Slogger. That will set us behind a bit. Then, when we come to bat I'll use some of the devil's potion. That should all be enough to ensure those Englishmen get their victory in Guyana."

The devil's potion – the mention of that made Rich start smiling.

"Do you have it with you, Rich?" asked Otis.

He looked at Rich and the big man held his belly and roared with laughter. Rich reached below the table for his briefcase. He turned the numbers of the combination lock to 666.666, and clicked the case open. He put his hand into the case and took out a clear plastic bag, which contained a white powder. He handed the bag to Otis.

"This will do the job," said Rich. "And make sure that Charlie Constantine gets more than his fair share. He is full of runs at the moment, and we can't have that now, can we? I've never liked him. Everyone thinks he's so lovely and marvellous."

"Tell me about it!" said Otis bitterly.

Rich started to laugh again, almost uncontrollably. He liked the devil's potion. He liked that very much indeed. It should stop that perfect gentleman and run glutton Charlie Constantine once and for all. Then he thought about all the money this would make him and laughed even louder.

"I would like to propose a toast," said Rich.

The other two raised their bottles of beer along with him.

"To an England victory," he said.

The three of them clinked their bottles and Rich Vermin started to laugh again. Then he began to sing.

"I'm in the money, I'm in the money," he bellowed in his tuneless and raucous voice.

The other two laughed nervously and hummed along to the tune with him.

Treasure Beach, Jamaica

"I can't face going to the game, FT," said Hurricane.

The boy looked forlorn.

"I know, son, I understand. I will let Mister Constantine know."

Charlie Constantine had kindly phoned to see if Hurricane wanted to travel with the team to Guyana, but the boy could not stand to watch a game he hoped he would have been playing in. Anyway, he and FT were due in court on the fourth day of the Test match for the hearing. It was a double blow.

"I think I'll just stay here and do some fishing and things," said Hurricane, morosely. "My only peace at the moment is out on the water in the boat."

6

The Devil's Potion

First Test at Bourda, Georgetown, Guyana
First Day

It was the predictable full house at Georgetown, Guyana for the game, the first Test of this much-hyped and eagerly-awaited five match series. Otis Campbell walked out to toss up with England captain Fitzwilliam Darcy. Darcy eyed the track approvingly – it was as flat as an ironing board, a perfect batting track, and the media pundits, especially with the absence of Hurricane Hamish from the West Indies team, were mostly predicting a draw.

What these television, radio and newspaper men did not know, however, was that Rich Vermin's plans were now in full operation. Otis had been arguing with the selectors all morning. They all had a preference for batting first if West Indies won the toss, but, in order to put his team at an immediate disadvantage, the crooked Otis had other ideas. He told a lie that he had spoken to the groundsman who said that if the pitch was to misbehave and help the bowlers it would do so on the first day. The groundsman, he said, had told him that the pitch would improve as the match went on. Reluctantly, though puzzled by this information, the selectors finally agreed. They were prepared to back their captain if he was so adamant.

So it was that Otis Campbell won the toss and decided to bowl. Fitzwilliam Darcy was more than delighted – above all else he had wanted first use of this wonderful track. Why would the West Indies choose to bowl, he wondered?

"Are you serious, Otis?" he said jokingly out there in the middle.

"Quite serious," said Otis with a glare.

Darcy shrugged and smiled and signalled a batting motion with his arm to the England manager Michael Atherton, who was up on the balcony of the England dressing-room.

Just before half-past ten, beneath a beautiful blue sky of the sort you only ever see in the Caribbean, Smithy the Slogger, helmetless as always, walked out to bat with Robert Martin, the solid Yorkshire left-hander. It might not have been Hurricane's début today, but Smith had the nod from the England selectors for his first Test. He had liked the look of the pitch when he had seen it this morning and could hardly believe his luck when Campbell chose to insert England.

The crowd was very noisy and fairly humming

with expectancy as Fish Archibald was marking out his run at the pavilion end. Otis Campbell ambled over to him, pretending to be nonchalant. Fish noticed that there was a strange distracted look on the captain's face. What was up?

"Fish. I'd like to save you for when some of the shine is off one side of the ball," said Otis. "You will get more movement then and perhaps some reverse swing. I'm going to open with Sherwin Padmore and Roy Amory."

The captain looked around at the field he had set and Fish could see that Otis would not meet his eye. Fish stared at him aghast. He had taken the new ball in every one of his previous ninety-five tests. Why this sudden change, especially when England had their new cap Smith coming in first?

"Surely not, skipper. We need to remove their young opener. He's dangerous," Fish said. "You have to let me have an early go at him, while the ball is hard."

"I'm in charge, Fish," said Otis with a raised voice, still not meeting his eye. "Take yourself down to long leg. Now."

He waved the fast bowler away.

Fish went and took his sweater from the umpire. A buzz of confusion went around the crowd. Fish was a hero throughout the Caribbean. For him not to be bowling the first over, as he always had done, was a shock to everybody. Over the last twelve years, the West Indian people had become used to and encouraged by the sight of Fish launching their attack on the opposition openers.

As bemused and unsettled as anyone, young Roy Amory, normally a first-change bowler, marked out his run in Fish's place and rubbed the brand-new cherry on his flannels. The crowd only began to settle down as Amory ran in to Smithy the Slogger.

Up on the dressing-room balcony, Vivian Richards was fuming. What was Otis doing? The chairman paced up and down cursing under his breath. This series was going to be hard enough to win without tactical errors like this. Curtly Ambrose and Courtney Walsh sat on the balcony as confused as the whole of the crowd. Brian Lara appeared at the door. He looked very perplexed and upset, and unusually for him there was no boyish smile on his face.

"Viv. Did you agree this with Otis? That he was not to use Fish with the new ball?"

"Of course not," said Richards. "I thought you must have done."

"No way," said Lara. "It's madness."

"Fish would be ideal to pressurize this new kid early on, to stop him from playing his shots," said Walsh.

The selectors looked to each other in turn for some sort of an explanation.

"What on earth's going on then?" asked Ambrose. "Smithy the Slogger will love this."

Indeed Smithy did. He smote Amory's third ball back over his head for six, and this gave him a surge of confidence which saw him launch a barrage of violent and powerful hitting against the West Indies opening pair. By the time Fish Archibald came on after an hour Smith already had 62 against his name. Most astonishingly of all, leg-spinner Larry King, against whom Smith was expected to be more vulnerable, did not bowl at all in the whole of the morning session, and by lunchtime England were a massive 161 for 0, Smith 102 not out – a rare and brutal Test century before lunch on his début.

By now the crowd was virtually silent and no-body enjoyed their lunch very much – except the England camp and the England supporters. Manager Atherton and Chairman Botham con-gratulated Smith and Robert Martin and told them to keep going. Rarely had the West Indies attack been so badly savaged and nobody could understand Otis Campbell's use – or misuse – of his bowlers.

After some strong words to him from Vivian Richards, Otis Campbell had no choice but to bring Larry King on straight after lunch, and the tall leg-spinner was straight into his rhythm on his home ground. He got Martin, Ferrers and Bingley in quick succession, but Smith managed to keep down the other end and continued to plunder runs from the quicker bowlers. Amazingly,

Campbell did nothing to change the field and try to force him to face more of King's deliveries.

To make matters worse, Smith smashed one ball so hard to cover that it split the spinning finger of Frankie Genus, the off-spinner who had come into the team in Hurricane's place. Genus left the field and would not bowl again in the match. The seamers were tiring and this allowed Smith and Knightley to put together a good partnership. This kept England well on top, although King managed to put some brake on the scoring rate.

Fish Archibald was bowling poorly, so upset was he by the events of the morning. His Jamaican colleague and captain, Charlie Constantine, could only look on bemused from his position at first slip. He watched the game with a captain's eye for tactics, being himself the experienced captain of Jamaica and the vice-captain of this team. What was Campbell doing today? Was he trying to lose them the game?

Tea came and went and long before the close a disappointed crowd had started to drift away from the ground. They had all bought their tickets in the hope of seeing Hurricane Hamish charge in on his début, and instead they had watched a novice English batsman plunder their attack. At the end of play England were 324 for 3, Smith 204 not out overnight, having reached his double century just before the close. Fish Archibald's figures for the day made sorry reading: 14-0-74-0. People could not remember him having bowled so badly.

Fish stood in the shower for a long time that night, waiting until most of the other players had left before emerging. He could not remember ever having been so angry and upset as he was today. He could not understand what was going on – and he knew that the West Indies would struggle to claw their way back from this position. He had never particularly rated Otis Campbell as a captain, but this was different – there was something almost deliberately damaging about the decisions Otis had made today.

Some of the men were in the bar having a drink. Fish was too upset to join them. He went straight back to the hotel. Later that night he watched the highlights of the game on the television in his room. He now saw for himself that he had never bowled that erratically for his country, so affected had he been by Otis's decisions and so shocked about not being given the new ball.

In his misery he still had time to spare a thought for Hurricane Hamish. What a different day it might have been if he had played! Fish eventually drifted off to sleep. He tossed and turned all night and had bad dreams about storms at sea.

Second Day

Larry King trapped Smith lbw early in the

morning with a googly. The generous Guyana crowd rose to the England opener – 214 in his first innings in Test cricket. It was a magnificent performance and he was applauded all the way back to the pavilion. Fish then bowled well all through the morning and early afternoon, well supported by Amory and Padmore, and by the middle of the second session England were all out – but they had 454 on the board, which was a formidable total.

The players left the field and Charlie Constantine hurried quickly up to the dressing-room. There were only ten minutes between innings and he liked to give himself as much time as possible to pad up and compose himself.

Otis Campbell was padding up across the other side of the dressing-room. As usual he and Charlie Constantine would open the innings together. When he was ready Otis came over to have a word with his vice-captain.

"You look a bit tired, Charlie," said Otis. "Here – have a spoonful of this glucose for some energy. I've just had some and it's done me the world of good."

He poured a sachet of the white powder into a glass of water for his opening partner and stirred it around with a spoon.

Charlie took the drink gratefully. He was indeed rather tired after a day and a half in the field and with only this very short time between innings to prepare himself for his batting. He wanted to make runs today – he knew he had a responsibility to his team to get the West Indies back in the game.

As they walked to the crease, however, Charlie began to feel a bit strange. He felt dizzy and slightly sick and was having trouble focusing. It was a swelteringly hot day again, but that did not explain why he was feeling like this.

Am I really that nervous? he thought. What's wrong with me?

Willoughby opened the bowling for England and he was feeling fast and fresh. As usual Charlie took the first delivery. The first ball whistled past Constantine's outside edge through to Churchill. The crowd drew breath. Charlie had hardly moved. His legs felt like lead and his mind seemed completely blank. He could not concentrate on the game and the job in hand. He looked around at the stands packed with people, but they were just one big blur and the ground was starting to spin.

The second ball from Willoughby was straighter and Charlie's bat was still waving around in the air when his off stump was plucked out of the ground. The crowd gasped and groaned. Charlie stared back at his stumps in horror – he could not understand it. Was he ill? He trooped off the field feeling desolate and very poorly. West Indies were 0 for 1.

The devil's potion had begun to work its spell and indeed Campbell had passed a few of the sachets around to his other key batsmen. He gave each of them a bit less than Constantine, so it took longer to take effect, but the West Indies top order came and went from the middle very quickly, as the world started to spin around about each of them after a short time at the crease.

Otis watched from the other end, scowling and pretending to be furious, but really smiling inside. The best batsmen were all soon back in the pavilion – Constantine for 0, Matthews for 12, James for 5, Goldman for 7, Alleyne for 3, King for 6. It was a disastrous end to the day for the West Indies. By the close they were 72 for 6, still 382 runs behind, Campbell 32 not out.

Third Day
Things did not last long on the next day. Otis used the devil's potion he had been given by Rich Vermin somewhat less on this third day of the match, but the damage had been done. All of the confidence and self-belief had drained out of the West Indies players and they seemed to have little spirit left for the fight. Campbell was last out for a very slow 39 and the West Indies were all out for only 94. Fitzwilliam Darcy had no hesitation in asking them to follow on and bat again.

Otis was not keen to use the potion too much, but he had promised Rich that he would use it on Charlie Constantine in both innings. He could not risk suspicion by offering Charlie a drink again, so he slipped some powder into some tea Charlie had left on the dressing-room table for a moment. He gave Charlie slightly less this time, accepting it would take a little longer to work.

Charlie was pleased to feel more like himself again as he walked out to bat. There was no way they would win from here, but he thought this match could be saved if only he could give the innings a sound basis by batting for a long time. He started well against Willoughby, cutting him past point for four and turning him off his legs through mid-wicket for two. He played some good shots against Wickham and soon he had 15 to his name. Yet, the illness, as he thought it was, started to come back.

At first it was just a slight blurring of vision, but soon the stands of people started to loom in on him. The sun seemed especially bright and the ground started to rock gently before him, working into a spin. He called to the dressing-room for some water and poured it over his head, but he still felt strange and the very next ball he chipped one from Wentworth straight to Smith at short mid-on.

West Indies had lost their backbone for the fight and everyone was deflated with Constantine's dismissal – he was, after all, the best batsman in the Caribbean. Otis got himself out quickly afterwards and the rest of the batting disinte-grated. With so many runs to play with, Darcy was able to put them under extreme pressure with aggressive field placing. The West Indies limped along to 145, but England took the last wicket just as the shadows were lengthening across the ground at the end of the day. They had beaten the West Indies within three days. England had won by an innings and 215 runs.

Over breakfast at the players' hotel the next morning, Fish Archibald was reading the papers. Needless to say, Rough Tungsten had a very different analysis of the match from that of the secret correspondent.

As a cover-up for the potion Rough Tungsten ran a story about the West Indies team suffering from upset stomachs. He also blamed their poor bowling and gutless batting in the second innings. He had been told by Rich to continue to cause havoc amongst the self-belief of the players and to use the newspaper to do so.

INCOMPETENCE SWEEPS
WEST INDIES CAMP

From our senior cricket reporter Rough Tungsten

The West Indies players really let their captain Otis Campbell down in the dreadful defeat at Georgetown yesterday. There was some illness amongst the West Indies players, probably caused by over-eating in the pre-match dinner, but this does not explain the total lack of support they gave their captain in their pathetic batting display. Charlie Constantine in particular seemed to think that it was a charity match rather than a Test match. He has made it clear to the selectors that his days playing at the top level are over...

Everything is an opinion, thought Fish Archibald, as he angrily put down the paper. He could not read any more of this clap-trap and it hurt him to see his long-time colleague Charlie Constantine so criticized. This Tungsten bloke seemed as though he had watched a different game from the one Fish played in.

He was pleased to see that *The Caribbean Chronicle* reported it rather differently.

CRAZY CAPTAINCY AS WEST INDIES CRASH

From The Caribbean Chronicle's secret correspondent

Some dreadful tactics and a mystery virus in the West Indies camp cost them the first Test at Georgetown. If Otis Campbell's captaincy was odd, the terrible dizziness affecting many of the West Indies batsmen was nothing short of suspicious...

Fish read through the article and agreed with every word. It had been an awful three days. Rarely had they been so humiliated by England. Yet something seemed to be not quite right. Like some of the other players, Fish felt a bit suspicious about the dizzy feelings so many of the batsmen had had. Yet no one seemed to be able to explain what could have caused it. It was too late now, anyway.

Still, he would be back home in Jamaica tomorrow. The trial about Hurricane Hamish's nationality and his rights to play for the West Indies was coming up. It seemed more important than ever that they get Hurricane into the team as soon as possible. They needed an injection of youthful enthusiasm. This match had been a total disaster – they needed Hurricane to be cleared to play for them and to come and help to turn the series around.

FIRST TEST SCORECARD

England

1st Innings

S T L Smith	lbw	b King	214
R Martin	c Archibald	b King	61
E S Ferrers		c & b King	9
C P Bingley	st Alleyne	b King	20
G Knightley	c Alleyne	b Archibald	73
F W Darcy*		b Padmore	0
E L Bertram	c Campbell	b Amory	17
F S Churchill+	lbw	b Padmore	20
F R Wentworth		b Archibald	4
G D Wickham		b Amory	8
J Willoughby		not out	5
Extras	(b8, lb9, nb6)		23

Total	**(all out)**	**454**

Fall of Wickets 1-174,2-189,3-220,4-340,5-369,
6-370,7-398,8-430,9-439,10-454

Bowling	O	M	R	W
R P B Amory	34.5	12	104	2
S T Padmore	25	4	100	2
F S Archibald	28	6	105	2
L V A King	45	14	122	4
F R Genus	3	0	6	0

West Indies

	1st Innings			*2nd Innings*		
C Constantine		b Willoughby	0	c Smith	b Wentworth	15
O K Campbell*		b Wickham	39	c Wentworth	b Wickham	15
R P Matthews	lbw	b Willoughby	12	c Churchill	b Bertram	28
J J James	c Darcy	b Wickham	5	lbw	b Bertram	1
B Goldman	c Darcy	b Wentworth	7	c Churchill	b Willoughby	24
A C Alleyne+	c Churchill	b Wickham	3		not out	40
L V A King	c Ferrers	b Willoughby	6		b Wentworth	13
S T Padmore		run out	7	c Smith	b Darcy	0
R P B Amory		b Wickham	0	c Churchill	b Darcy	3
F S Archibald	lbw	b Bertram	10	lbw	b Bertram	0
F R Genus		not out	0		b Willoughby	0
Extras	(b3, lb2)		5	(b1, lb3, nb2)		6

Total	**(all out)**	**94**	**(all out)**	**145**

Fall of Wickets 1-0,2-20,3-30,4-39,5-49,   1-31,2-34,3-42,4-81,5-102,
6-61,7-76,8-76,9-90,10-94   6-123,7-129,8-134,9-138,10-145

Bowling	O	M	R	W	O	M	R	W
J Willoughby	16	6	20	3	19.3	4	55	2
G D Wickham	10	4	31	4	15	5	25	1
F R Wentworth	9	0	27	1	14	4	28	2
E L Bertram	13	8	11	1	8	1	24	3
F W Darcy	4	4	0	0	6	4	9	2

Man of the Match: S T L Smith (England)
England won by an innings and 215 runs

7

Silence in Court

The courthouse, Kingston, Jamaica

The courthouse in Kingston was packed to the rafters. The Test match had finished prematurely, so the Jamaican people were no longer glued to their television sets. They had all come to court instead. After such an appalling defeat, everybody was debating more eagerly than ever whether Hurricane would live out his destiny to be a West Indies player, or whether this would be denied him. The team seemed to need him.

Clearly this court case was about two things. First of all it was about whether two people who loved each other – Hurricane Hamish and FT – could stay together. Secondly it was about Hurricane's right to call himself a West Indian, and therefore about the future health of West Indies cricket. It was a private drama and a public drama all rolled into one, and everybody had an opinion and everybody was keen to witness the outcome. So the courthouse was packed.

Hurricane sat with FT and Wesley Clarke at the

front of the courtroom facing the bench where the notorious judge would sit. For they were all waiting for Judge Herring – the lawyer with the reputation as the hard man of Jamaican justice.

Hurricane looked absurd in an ill-fitting suit he had borrowed from Wesley Clarke, which was far too small for him. The jacket only came down to his forearms and the trouser hems flapped around his shins. He wore the tie of the Jamaican cricket team. FT was wearing his only suit, dressed very sombrely all in black, looking as if he was attending a funeral. Wesley Clarke wore a normal suit, too, not looking himself without the police uniform which everybody was accustomed to seeing him in. He was barred from wearing it for now.

It was hot in court. The electric fans whirred overhead, but many of the people were also fanning themselves with the books or newspapers they had with them. Hurricane was fanning himself with *The Caribbean Chronicle* – he liked to have the secret correspondent as close to him as possible. For, increasingly, the secret correspondent seemed to be becoming his friend and his champion.

In the back row of court, hiding away in a corner, sat Rich Vermin. He was eating a huge bar of chocolate and fanning himself with *The West Indies Wayfarer*. He was very pleased with a one-nil score in the Test series, but knew he had to keep Hurricane out of things for as long as possible. He was probably the only person in court not to be on Hurricane's side.

There was an air of expectancy in the room.

"All rise," someone suddenly shouted, and the people rose as one as the judge breezed into the courtroom from a door at the back.

Judge Herring was a big, ferocious-looking man with lots of grey hair in dreadlocks and a huge white beard. He wore a long and flowing black cape.

He waved his arms, motioning the people back on to their chairs.

"The court will be seated," he called out.

He remained standing himself for a few moments and surveyed the court, as the people settled back into their seats. It had not been like this for some time, not an empty chair to be seen. They were so crushed in up on the balcony, there were people standing. His eyes were drawn to the front row of seats, and he looked at the witnesses lined up there. They shared a look of some fear and much sadness.

An attendant approached the bench and spoke quietly with the judge. He was a young man, who then turned and faced the court and addressed the audience.

"The court calls Wesley Clarke."

Wesley approached the witness box which was close to the judge's bench, and which was turned to face the court. As he walked up there he felt naked in his clothes, conscious of the shame of the suspension which had cost him his uniform.

The attendant brought him a Bible and Wesley swore the oath to tell the truth to the court. Judge Herring looked across at him. He knew of Wesley, knew of him as a model police officer and citizen. He had dealt with him in previous legal cases and had been impressed. He was surprised at his involvement in this particular story.

"Officer Clarke," he said.

"Yes, Your Honour?" replied Wesley. He was gulping nervously.

"Officer Clarke. Perhaps we can avoid a lot of questions by me, and you can just tell us in your own words how we all come to be here. What happened with regard to this young man," and he pointed to Hurricane, "those many years ago? What was the part you played in it?"

Wesley looked out at the crowd gathered in the many seats before him. He felt the sympathy in all of their eyes, which gave him the strength to talk.

He told the tale of what had happened all those years ago in the days after the storm which had kept everyone in their homes. He talked over the incident in great depth. He told of how FT had brought the child to the police station. He told of the visit of the fat woman from social services. He told of his instincts and feelings. He told of how he had hidden the file – and with it the MCC towel – and how he had forged the papers for FT. He told of how he had fixed it for the old man to keep the child. He told the whole truth.

The MCC towel was brought to him as Exhibit A in the case. Wesley looked at it and confirmed that it was the towel which he had kept hidden in his filing cabinet for all those years.

"That's it," he said, handing the towel back to the attendant. "That's the towel FT found the boy in. It was in my cabinet with the secret file. How did it reach the court?"

"It was sent to us anonymously," said the attendant.

Rich Vermin suppressed a giggle. Tungsten had done his job for once.

The attendant passed the towel to Judge Herring who turned it over carefully in his hands, inspecting the MCC letters which were embroidered in gold.

Wesley had finished his tale and he realized that everybody in the courthouse was staring at him. The crowd had hung on his every word and as he stopped speaking people shuffled in their seats and there were mutterings of approval and support.

Judge Herring coughed and wrote something down. Then he addressed Wesley. His voice was severe.

"Tell me, Officer Clarke. You are a respected and long-serving policeman. You are a student of the law of the island. You are fully aware of all administrative procedure regarding orphan children. What on earth led you to do this?"

Wesley bowed his head in the witness box, thinking. He closed his eyes and rubbed the bridge of his nose thoughtfully. He mopped his brow with his blue-spotted handkerchief. Then he raised his head and looked the judge straight in the eye. Herring met his gaze and spoke again.

"Answer the question, Officer Clarke. Are you aware of the size of the crime you committed – however long ago it may have been? Do you know how serious this is? Where would we be if everyone like you decided to take such matters into their own hands?"

The people in the court shifted in their seats, waiting.

Still fixing his gaze on Judge Herring, Wesley spoke very calmly and clearly.

"In thirty years as a policeman, I've always performed my duties to the letter of the law. I did this one thing which was outside the law. I believe, however, that my reasons were sound."

Herring frowned.

"And what, sir, were those reasons? I would remind you that you are under oath."

The judge's voice was raised.

"Judge Herring, sir," said Wesley, still very calmly. "It was a matter of right and wrong."

"How do you mean, Officer Clarke? Right

and wrong? The court would welcome an explanation."

"Well," said Wesley. "I knew that procedure would deny the chance for the right thing to be done. I knew – don't ask me how, but I just knew – that for the boy to stay with that man over there who found him..."

He pointed to FT and smiled at his friend. FT was chewing a matchstick nervously.

"...I knew it was the right thing. It was meant to be. And do you see the way they are together now, the fine way the boy has been brought up, his charming character, his sense of fun and freedom, his love for the world around him. I was right."

The people of the court sighed in a sort of general agreement. Some people were nodding.

"And, sir," he continued. "I don't care what this court decides – you part that boy and that man and you are doing WRONG. Sometimes the law is an ass. Sometimes rules are there to be broken. Maybe just once in a lifetime, but sometimes a man's feeling and instincts tell a truer story than any of your laws."

Wesley went silent. The whole courtroom held its breath, in awe at the man's words, at his courage before the terrifying judge. The only sound was the tap of the computer as the clerk recorded every word. Everybody was staring at Judge Herring to see his reaction. Judge Herring was staring at Wesley Clarke. Eventually the judge spoke.

"Thank you very much, Officer Clarke. You may step down now."

So quiet was the courtroom, that you could hear the echo of Wesley's steps as he returned to his seat. As Wesley sat down next to him, FT gripped his arm and gave it a squeeze of thanks. He knew once and for all that Wesley was prepared to risk his whole career for him and the boy.

FT was next into the witness box. The old man looked very tired as he took the Bible in his hand and uttered the oath. This trouble over Hurricane was hurting him so much. The issue of whether Hurricane could play for the cricket team was one thing, but there was so much more at stake. The thought of losing the boy made him feel empty inside and half dead. Cricket was one thing, but this was about their lives, their everyday existence.

As he stood there his mind drifted away. He could not live without the boy running back wet from the beach, after body-surfing the waves; he could not live without the boy telling him about the fishing catch and how the water was today on the Pedro Banks; he could not live without the boy shaking him awake every morning, singing: "Wakey, wakey FT. I'm off to catch some fish for our breakfast, old man." He could just about live without the boy playing cricket for the West Indies but he could not live without these things.

FT was miles away, lost in his troubles as he sat there. He had not heard the judge's question.

"Witness. Did you hear me?" asked Judge Herring.

"I'm so sorry," said FT. "Could you repeat the question, Your Honour?"

"Could you tell me a little about what the two of you – you and the boy, Hurricane Hamish – do in your everyday lives?"

FT spoke very quietly and his voice was cracking. He was struggling to hold his emotions together. He was too upset to look over at Hurricane. He spoke briefly of the house and the beach and the simple lives they led, and Hurricane's constant cricketing. The court was enraptured as he spoke of their lives together, a straightforward tale of two people who wanted for nothing more.

"And school, sir?" asked Judge Herring. "Does the boy go to school?"

"No, Your Honour. I taught him myself," said FT.

"The boy can read and write then?" asked the judge.

"He can," said FT, proudly. "And much more besides."

"You have no plans on him getting any school qualifications, though?" asked the judge in exasperation.

"That's up to Hurricane. He says he'll be a fisherman, or even better he'll play cricket for a living. If it wasn't for all of this nonsense it was starting to look as though he had a real chance of doing that, as well. To play cricket for your country beats anything you learn at school."

A murmur of approval went around the people in the courthouse.

"Quiet," called out Judge Herring, angrily. "I will have silence in my court."

He glared across the sea of faces.

"And this boy fishes alone, you say?"

"Yes, sir," said FT.

"How old is the boy?" asked the judge.

FT was silent.

"I must remind you, sir, that you are under oath."

FT looked across at the judge. This is going badly, he thought. Still, the truth is the truth. There's no hiding from that.

"When I found him he was very tiny – must have been only days old. That was twelve years and nine months ago."

A gasp went around the courthouse. Herring glared around at them and, as one, the people went silent.

"I'm most perplexed by your attitude in raising this child," said the judge. "A twelve-year-old who doesn't go to school and goes fishing the Pedro Banks alone. Very interesting. Very interesting indeed. How do you explain it?"

"Well," said FT. "It doesn't matter what it is – fishing, cricket, anything. What I always say is that if you're good enough, you're old enough."

The court was still. Judge Herring was writing things down again.

"No more questions. The witness will step down please," he said.

With his head bowed, FT walked back to his seat. He felt he had got it all wrong, but what was he to say? How was he to explain to this judge that he and Hurricane were just fine. They lived in their own way, but they wanted for nothing and they had each other. Anyone who knew him could see what a happy kid Hurricane was. He just wanted to play cricket.

The attendant came and spoke to the judge again. The attendant turned to the court.

"The court calls Hurricane Hamish," he said.

As he stood in the box, Hurricane felt very nervous. He looked up into the gallery. He did not recognize too many of the faces, these kind faces of people who were on his side. Yet, suddenly, one face in particular caught his eye.

The mystery girl was here, back in his life again. Who was she? What was she here for?

He felt different when he saw her. Her presence made him feel calm. He felt a new strength inside him – a situation that had been desperate now seemed so simple.

"Do you have anything to add to what has been

said?" Judge Herring asked him, jolting him back to the matter in hand.

"Yes, sir," said Hurricane.

"Proceed then," said the judge impatiently. "Then I will ask you some questions."

"What I have to say is this," said Hurricane. He looked up again to the balcony and the mystery girl met his eyes.

"I am happy," he began. "I have all I need. I have always been well looked after. I have never wanted for love. A kid knows inside him where he belongs. I belong with FT."

He smiled at the old man and pointed him out proudly to the whole of the court.

"It's very simple, Judge Herring, sir. We're a team now. We need each other. Your rules don't understand that. I belong here. I am Jamaican. I know it. After all, it's me we're talking about. If you understood anything, you would sign some papers and just let me go back to the life I love. That, sir, is what I have to say."

The court was hushed. Even the clocks seemed to stop ticking. Time stood still. All eyes flicked from Hurricane to Judge Herring, from Judge Herring back to Hurricane. Everyone was waiting for the reaction of the judge.

The judge coughed. He was slightly red in the face. He was angered at the child's defiance, but impressed too by the strength of his words. He was confused by this whole case, as well. The law said one thing, but somehow his heart was telling him something else. This made him even more baffled and angry. He would just have to throw it out of court for a while and give himself some breathing space and thinking time.

"You may step down," he said to Hurricane.

Judge Herring was still writing. Then he raised his head from his papers. Hurricane was still standing in the dock.

"I shall reconvene the court at a later date to ask you some more detailed questions. I said that you may step down."

Surprised, Hurricane returned to his seat. Judge Herring started writing again and the people in the courthouse waited to see what he had to say. Eventually he rose to his feet and addressed them.

"I cannot grant custody, citizenship, any papers of residency or West Indian rights until this issue is resolved," said Judge Herring. "This unique case requires more time to investigate the appearance of Hurricane Hamish in Jamaica twelve years ago, and more time for anyone with a claim to be his parents to present themselves. I do not intend to drag this out, however. We will adjourn for ten days when the court will reconvene. At that point the court will ask Hurricane Hamish some more detailed questions and the court will make a decision."

Everybody sighed, somewhat confused at this lack of conclusion. A whisper went around the people in the court: "Not a bad outcome. Judge

Herring is playing for time. Hurricane will miss the next Test, though."

The Conch Bar, Kingston, Jamaica

The bar was more gloomy than ever. The three villains huddled around their usual table, hidden away in the shadowy corner of the room.

Rich Vermin fiddled with the combination on the black briefcase. Rough Tungsten and Otis Campbell watched him warily. Rich enjoyed playing with the number dial, and bringing up his secret code: 666.666. He clicked the case open.

Immediately there was a dazzling kaleidoscope of rays of light. The bar room lamps played on the objects in the case and Otis and Rough watched as the patterns of reflected light danced around Rich Vermin's face. He laughed and the effect of the jigging flashes on his gold front teeth made him look more scary than ever.

He withdrew the objects from the case. Rough and Otis stared down at his hands. He held a number of small mirrors, and different patterns of light started to shimmer all around the bar on to the walls and ceiling. Rich Vermin started to laugh again.

He looked at Rough and Otis. The light bouncing off his teeth nearly blinded them as Rich Vermin chanted: "Mirror, mirror on the wall. Who is the richest of us all?"

8

Magic Mirrors

Second Test at The Queen's Park Oval, Port-of-Spain, Trinidad

First Day

Rough Tungsten liked Trinidad. He had drafted a clever article about the island, explaining to the readers that Columbus discovered it on his third voyage in 1498. It is the southernmost of the Caribbean islands, just north of the coast of Venezuela, and certainly one of the most colourful.

Rough had written all this stuff because Rich Vermin had ordered him to try to distract his readers. Rich was very irritated that everyone was still talking about the trial and that Hurricane Hamish kid. The longer he could be kept in the wilderness the more chance Rough, Rich and Otis had of seeing this England victory through and taking their money home.

Rough looked out across The Queen's Park Oval. It was not a bad way to earn loads of money from Rich Vermin and pay off his debts –

keeping a watchful eye on the cricket in a beautiful setting like this.

Out in the middle Otis was with Fitzwilliam Darcy for the toss. Darcy stared quizzically at the pitch. It was like Trinidad pitches always were these days – a strip of parched earth, simply rolled mud left to dry which looked a bit like an oblong of badly-laid cement. He thought that Larry King might bowl well on it for the West Indies and he thought it would get slower and lower as the game wore on. England had decided on two spinners – medium-pacer Wentworth making way for the left-armer Henry Tilney. Darcy would act as the third seamer himself. Despite the débâcle at Georgetown, the West Indies team was unchanged.

With the balance towards spin in his side, and with West Indies playing two slow bowlers as well, Darcy's preference was to bat first as in the first Test. This would mean that England would take the first and third innings of the game and would not be facing King at the end of the match in the fourth innings, when their own spinners might get some help from the wicket. He was therefore very surprised when once again Campbell invited England to bat first.

"You sure, Otis?" Darcy joked.

Again all he got from Otis was that increasingly familiar glare.

The day ran its natural course (as the three villains had accepted it should if England batted first), which made a change for the crowd after the tumble of wickets and very fast scoring in the first Test. The only notable thing on this flat track was some rather overly attacking fields from Otis Campbell, which meant England scored more quickly than they might have done throughout this first day.

Fish Archibald was back in his rhythm and bowling well again. Even so, things looked ominous for the West Indies in the first hour, as Smith, who was full of confidence after the first Test, made a very quick fifty. He looked dangerous until Fish moved one away from him and had him caught behind by Andy Alleyne. The rest of the England order batted solidly, held together by a long and painstaking innings from left-handed opener Rob Martin, who missed out on a century when he offered a return catch to the off-spinner Genus just before the close. The other batsmen forced the pace, but the middle order proved flash rather than reliable and England wickets fell regularly throughout the day. Larry King picked up four of them, bowling unchanged through the afternoon and evening sessions, and he was well supported by Frankie Genus, who bowled very tidily.

By the close of play, it had been a fairly even day, with West Indies perhaps slightly on top.

England had scored 285 for 8. Rough wrote his article, criticizing the West Indies for lack-lustre bowling. He had enjoyed an entertaining day's play, made all the more sweet by the prospect of the role he was due to play in the match tomorrow. It was time to perform some magic with the tiny mirrors.

Second Day

In the morning the England late order did not last long. Genus picked up the wickets of Churchill and Willoughby and England were all out for 292. It was time for Rough Tungsten to go into action.

Rough was in the perfect spot for today's plan. He hid in one of the cubicles of the toilet of the press box with the mirrors he needed. No one could see him here. It was another of Rich Vermin's rather extreme ideas, but Rough was happy to try anything to help get his money. He chuckled to himself. Charlie Constantine would be his first victim. Rough was going to ruin Charlie's day, that was for sure.

Between innings Rough had got his angles sorted out. The sun reflected off the specially-shaped mirror and out of the toilet window. A dot of light appeared at the edge of the square. Rough played around with it, moving it around to get the feel for his equipment. He needed to be able to blind the batsman in a brief instant, by fixing a tiny but dazzlingly bright ray in his eyes just as the bowler released the ball. He had to take his hat off to Rich Vermin – this was the best plan yet.

After his disappointing 0 and 15 at Georgetown, Charlie was more determined than ever to make an impact on the game today. He had read the articles in *The West Indies Wayfarer* by Rough Tungsten after that game, saying that his Test match days were behind him. After that article, mutterings had started in other quarters that Charlie's reactions were starting to fail him and that he no longer had the stamina to bat for long periods in the Caribbean heat. Charlie knew in his own mind that it was something else. He had felt ill in those two innings.

He walked out to bat more determined than he had ever been. He and Otis rarely talked much, but on the way to the middle Charlie spoke to him.

"I'm going to get you some runs today, Otis," he said.

"Good," said Otis, gruffly. "You owe the side some. If not we'll have to think about giving young Radwick Scorpio a chance."

Charming, thought Charlie. Radwick Scorpio was a talented young opener for Trinidad, twelfth man again today, who some were advocating for the Test team in Charlie's place.

Inside Otis was laughing. Poor, determined Charlie. Little did he know what was in store for him.

Charlie took his usual guard – leg stump. Willoughby was marking out his run. Charlie took a wander down the pitch to study it. The wicket should not provide too many problems early on, he thought, and he had a good record here in Trinidad – he had made lots of runs here before. He settled into his stance and waited for the first delivery.

Willoughby charged in and let one go – a short one. Charlie saw it well and got straight on to the back foot to get into line early. Then something bizarre happened. He was half-way through his stroke and a great flash of white light seemed to smash its way into his brain. He never got himself into any position to play a shot and the ball whistled past his right ear and flew into Frank Churchill's gloves behind the wicket. Charlie was lucky it did not take his head off.

Willoughby stared down the track, delighted but surprised. He had never seen this from Constantine – had never seen him flinch from the bowling like that.

Charlie was totally confused about what was going on. What was the matter with him? After the sickness in the first Test what were these sudden flashes of light? He sensed the tension around the ground as the whole crowd was silent with shock.

Willoughby ran in again. Just as he let go of the ball a white flash exploded through Charlie's eyes and head again, almost sending a jerk through his whole body. All he heard was a gasp and a groan from the crowd. As his sight slowly returned he looked back at his stumps in disbelief. His middle stump was pegged back. Willoughby was running past him down the pitch to celebrate with the other England players. It had happened again. Bowled for a duck.

Up in his cubicle Rough laughed out loud as Charlie walked off the ground to complete silence. Between them he, Otis and Rich were destroying Charlie's Test career – and the West Indies had depended on him as the cornerstone of their batting for so long.

The trick had worked perfectly, but the villains were not going to push their luck. The agreement had been to use the mirrors sparingly to avoid excessive suspicion. Rough used them twice more in the day – and helped in the dismissals of two of the key batsmen, Joel James and Brian Goldman. With Constantine, James and Goldman looking so strangely vulnerable, the rest of the batting was low on confidence. Otis deliberately got himself out for 20 and, despite some resistance from Matthews, Alleyne and King, nobody really got going throughout the day. West Indies were all out in the final session for only 187. By the close England had comfortably eased along to 53 for 0, increasing their lead to 158.

Third Day

The third day belonged to the spinners, the pitch already turning a little and offering some help to the experienced Larry King. He bowled quite beautifully and had good support once again from the young off-spinner Frankie Genus. England struggled against the slow bowling all day. Smith was first out in the second over of the day for 34 and though some of the England players got decent starts, they scratched their way through each of the three sessions. King bowled a couple of long spells and for extended periods he and Genus made it an all-spin attack. England added only 231 in the day and lost nine wickets to be 284 for 9 at stumps.

At the close, with two days remaining, England were 389 ahead with only one wicket left. It seemed the West Indies might have an outside chance – but, for reasons no one in the Caribbean except the three villains understood, they seemed incapable at the moment of putting a decent total together.

Fourth Day

Rough Tungsten woke up to rain beating down on the press hotel window. When it rains in Port-of-Spain it really does rain. The ground was awash when he arrived and Rough sat for several hours up in the press box feeling very frustrated, watching the streams of water wash over the huge glass window.

He needed the players back out there. England had to win this Test. That would give them a two-nil advantage in the series which the West Indies would really struggle to reverse. It was so frustrating, because he had been looking forward to another day's selective use of the mirrors.

Alone in the press box he stared out at the rain. He was just thinking about going back to the hotel when the phone went.

"Hello. Press box," he said.

"Tungsten!" someone shouted.

There was no doubting who it was – Rough would recognize that voice anytime.

"Hello, Rich. Shame about the rain."

"A shame. It's a disaster. You should have had the game over by now," Rich bellowed down the phone.

"But, you said..."

"Don't tell me what I did or did not say, Tungsten. We can't allow a draw in this match. Now listen. Tomorrow it's going to start fine. Between the two of you, Campbell and you have got to get this game over – but make it look authentic. There are already too many rumours going around about Constantine, James and Goldman having been blinded by something strange in the first innings. Only use the mirrors as and when you have to, you fool. With one exception. Get rid of Constantine early. I want to see him bag his first pair in Test cricket. That should get him dropped for the next one."

Rough could hear Rich Vermin laughing.

"West Indies might fold on their own, they're so rattled by what's been happening. If not – just get those little beauties out and do your stuff. Understood!"

The phone buzzed in Rough's ear. Rich Vermin had hung up.

Rough silently made a wish for a sunny day tomorrow.

Fifth Day

Rough woke up to a beautiful, dazzling Caribbean morning, and when he got to the ground he did his experiments to make sure he had the angles right for the mirrors. However, he noticed some clouds looming off in the distance. He had a lot to do today – and he needed the sunshine to do it.

England helped by declaring their innings closed. They wanted to give themselves the whole day to try to bowl the West Indies out and they were a comfortable 389 runs ahead.

Charlie Constantine was perhaps more nervous than he had been in the whole of his long and illustrious West Indies career. Otis had told him again that morning that his place was in jeopardy and he could feel the weight of expectation upon him. One more failure and he might lose his place to young Radwick Scorpio.

The crowd applauded him and Otis on to the ground. As usual, Charlie would take the first ball.

Willoughby was looking keen, boosted by his 3 for 45 in the first innings and the knowledge that Constantine had seemed to flinch away from his bowling.

Up in the toilet cubicle Rough had Charlie in his sights. Rough waited for four balls – and indeed Charlie looked very comfortable, letting the first two pass harmlessly outside off stump and playing two immaculate forward defensive strokes to the next two. The crowd was settling down, hoping that the West Indies could bat this comfortably all day for the draw.

The fifth delivery was a fast in-swinging yorker. As he saw the ball curve in, Charlie's movement was suddenly frozen as the world became one big, bright white sabre of light and the pain of this momentary blindness seared through his skull. He cried out in anguish, but only together with the sound of the ball hitting the base of the leg stump and the great groan of the crowd coming across the ground. Charlie stood there in disbelief. He could not understand how this had happened again – bowled Willoughby 0 – a pair in the match, his first pair in Tests.

He walked off totally bemused. Where had that flash come from? What was happening to him in this series? He considered briefly that he might be going mad.

Otis got himself out in Willoughby's next over, deliberately shuffling across and missing a straight one to be caught plumb lbw. West Indies had had the worst possible start – 10 for 2. Matthews and James dug in, however, and managed to see the side through to lunch, when the score was 61 for 2.

Rough had not resorted to the magic mirrors again, but over lunch he was concerned by the clouds, which now seemed to be heading towards the ground. Without sun, he would not be able to use the mirrors. He decided he must act quickly before the chance escaped him.

A blinding flash greeted each of Matthews, James and Alleyne in the first half-hour after lunch and their blind jerky shots saw England reduce the West Indies to 88 for 5. Rough started to relax – surely that was the end. Of the recognized batsmen, only Goldman and King were left. He could forget the mirrors now and enjoy watching England run through the West Indies tail. He settled back in his chair behind his computer.

Rough got so relaxed he dozed off. He dreamt that he was sailing out on the Caribbean Sea in a huge yacht with Rich Vermin and Otis Campbell, sipping a dark rum cocktail and sunning himself out on deck.

He only woke to frantic cheering. He looked over the ground. Everyone was standing and applauding – 50 to Brian Goldman. He and King were going along very well and what was even worse for Rough, the sun was in behind the clouds, and the mirrors were useless for now.

The two batsmen progressed nicely, batting to try to last the day and get the draw, but picking off any runs as and when they could, taking advantage of Darcy's attacking fields. Rough peered desperately up at the sky. The clouds were moving over the ground, and there was bright weather behind them, but would the sun come out soon enough?

Tea came and went, before too long King reached 50 and, an hour later, with only a few overs left in the day the crowd rose as one to acclaim a beautifully crafted century from the Antiguan Brian Goldman.

Yet, at the moment Goldman took off his helmet and raised his bat to acclaim the applause, the sun came out again. Rough was already back in his cubicle. Willoughby was operating from this end, the one from which Rough could use the mirrors. Time was very, very short though – only two overs left before the close. He had to do the damage in this over. He just hoped that Willoughby would bowl straight.

Willoughby ran in and bowled, digging in a shorter one. The light flashed through Goldman's head, his body jerked, the ball hit the shoulder of his bat and flew over the slips for four. Larry King walked down the pitch to talk to him.

"You OK, Brian? What happened there?"

"I don't know. I just got one of those bright light flashes like I got in the first innings. You know – like the ones which Charlie and some of the others have been talking about. I don't know what on earth's going on."

Goldman was rubbing his eyes.

"Try to ignore it," said Larry King. "We can't do anything. Nothing looks amiss behind the bowler's arm. Keep going. We've only got a couple of overs to survive. We're nearly there."

Brian Goldman nodded, returned to the crease and settled into his stance to face Willoughby again.

Come on, he said to himself. Just a couple more overs.

They were hopeless words though. For the next ball Goldman was blinded again and only managed a thin edge to the wicket-keeper – and the astonishing procession began.

242 for 6.

Willoughby bowled an in-swinger to Padmore which took leg stump as stars exploded around the batsman's brain.

242 for 7.

Willoughby bowled a straight one to Amory who staggered across his stumps in his blindness and was given out lbw.

242 for 8.

Willoughby plucked off Fish Archibald's off bail as Fish's head swam and he flailed a hopeless bat at the ball.

242 for 9.

Frankie Genus missed Willoughby's leg stump

yorker as what seemed like a laser beam rocketed through his head.

242 all out.

The West Indies players sat around the dressing-room in a stunned silence. They had collapsed from 242 for 5 to 242 all out in one over from Willoughby. The men involved were complaining bitterly of a funny blinding sensation as they were trying to play their shots. Charlie Constantine nodded in understanding. Something very strange had been happening in this match and he was beginning to suspect some foul play. Otis was ranting at his players, pretending to be angry and accusing them of making excuses for their cowardice against Willoughby's pace.

In the England dressing-room John Willoughby was sitting quietly sipping a glass of champagne, trying to take it all in. Five wickets in five balls to take England to a stunning and unexpected victory with just minutes to spare. He had never managed anything like it before, and he could not believe the way the West Indies players had seemed to flinch at the crease.

Outside the ground Rough Tungsten walked along the Port-of-Spain streets. He had already rung in his report to *The West Indies Wayfarer*. *WEST INDIES SCARED OF WILLOUGHBY* had been his headline. He fingered the mirrors in his jacket pocket and whistled a tune.

The Conch Bar, Kingston, Jamaica

Rich Vermin parked the black van in the street and hurried into The Conch Bar. The English couple were already sitting there. They certainly looked the part, all forlorn and somehow homely. These two were ideal, thought Rich. There they were – right on time and sitting at the right table.

"Now then, now then," he said, greeting them warmly and pumping their hands enthusiastically. Rich Vermin could be very polite when he wanted to be, very smarmy and sickening indeed.

Rich Vermin motioned over to the bar. The barman came over to take their order. The couple ordered rum and Rich Vermin ordered himself a beer. He sat across the table staring at them. For all their ordinariness, close up he could see that both the man and the woman had evil, greedy eyes. Rich Vermin liked to see that in people he worked with. They were his sort of people.

"Now listen," said Rough. "The court will be packed on Saturday. We need you to walk in, very dramatically, waving the birth certificate and that MCC towel I sent to you. Everything will stop.

"There will then just be a need for one or two more decisions from that Herring bloke. The boy will be confirmed as belonging to you and unable to play for the West Indies.

"Before you can say Jack Robinson, we'll have played the third Test and the series will be all over, without that lanky child having even bowled a single ball. There's something really rather perfect about all this, don't you think?"

They talked about the plan for the courthouse in more detail, but eventually, getting impatient, the couple wanted to see some of what they had come for.

"Let's see the money," said the man. "Before we go any further."

Rich Vermin looked around furtively. The bar was deserted except for a young girl who was sitting alone by the door.

Rich took a huge wad of notes from his pocket and counted them out on the table. When he had finished, he rather dramatically pulled a briefcase from under the table and fiddled with the combination to bring up 666.666. He clicked it open.

"And all the rest of this will be yours," he said, showing the contents of the case to the couple. "That is if you do the job and if you do not mess it up. OK?"

The two of them looked greedily at the money in the case. The man licked his tongue around his lips. He had never seen so much money in his life. This bloke Rich Vermin really was something.

Rich snapped the case shut. The three of them rose from their seats and shuffled out of the bar.

When they had gone, and while the barman was briefly down in the beer cellar, the girl who had been sitting at the table by the door got up. She went over to the table Rich Vermin and the English couple had just left. She reached underneath it and started to release something which had been concealed under there. She smiled — now at last was a chance to put a stop to this plotting against Hurricane Hamish.

SECOND TEST SCORECARD

England

	1st Innings				2nd Innings		
S T L Smith	c Alleyne	b Archibald	55	lbw		b Amory	34
R Martin		c & b Genus	98	c King		b Genus	20
E S Ferrers	c Constantine	b Amory	36			run out	6
C P Bingley	lbw	b King	16	c Padmore		b King	56
G Knightley	c Genus	b King	21			b King	23
F W Darcy*		b Archibald	25	c Matthews		b Genus	42
E L Bertram	c James	b King	9	lbw		b King	15
F S Churchill+		b Genus	9	c Matthews		b Amory	0
H P A Tilney		b King	12	c Alleyne		b King	49
G D Wickham		not out	0			not out	21
J Willoughby	lbw	b Genus	0			not out	8
Extras	(b2, lb3, nb6)		11	(b5, nb4 w1)			10

Total   **(all out)**   **292**   **(for 9 declared)**   **284**

Fall of Wickets   1-85,2-134,3-174,4-210,5-241   1-54,2-58,3-70,4-145,5-176,
6-251,7-265,8-284,9-292,10-292   6-191,7-199,8-209,9-253

Bowling	O	M	R	W	O	M	R	W
F S Archibald	22	7	59	2	16	2	34	0
R P B Amory	12	0	57	1	14	2	40	2
S T Padmore	13	0	45	0	10	0	41	0
L V A King	27	7	89	4	39	19	97	4
F R Genus	20.3	9	37	3	28	10	67	2

West Indies

	1st Innings				2nd Innings		
C Constantine		b Willoughby	0			b Willoughby	0
O K Campbell*	lbw	b Wickham	20	lbw		b Willoughby	4
R P Matthews	c Darcy	b Bertram	39			b Bertram	32
J J James		b Willoughby	2	c Churchill		b Darcy	24
B Goldman	c Churchill	b Darcy	7	c Churchill		b Willoughby	104
A C Alleyne+	c Tilney	b Darcy	36	lbw		b Wickham	8
L V A King	lbw	b Tilney	38			not out	67
S T Padmore		not out	18			b Willoughby	0
R P B Amory		b Bertram	0	lbw		b Willoughby	0
F S Archibald	c Knightley	b Bertram	10			b Willoughby	0
F R Genus		c & b Willoughby	4			b Willoughby	0
Extras	(b3, lb3, nb3, w4)		13	(lb3)			3

Total   **(all out)**   **187**   **(all out)**   **242**

Fall of Wickets   1-0,2-46,3-61,4-74,5-112,   1-0,2-10,3-61,4-62,5-88,
6-125,7-149,8-149,9-177,10-187   6-242,7-242,8-242,9-242,10-242

Bowling	O	M	R	W	O	M	R	W
J Willoughby	14.4	4	45	3	16	4	41	7
G D Wickham	13	6	50	1	17	1	59	1
F W Darcy	17	3	44	2	25	6	78	1
E L Bertram	15	5	32	3	17	7	41	1
H P A Tilney	13	8	10	1	14	4	20	0

Man of the Match: J Willoughby (England)
England won by 147 runs

9

Judge Herring Decides

The courthouse, Kingston, Jamaica

The ten days had passed. It was not particularly surprising to see that once again the court was heaving with people. There were hundreds more outside who had not been able to get in. People had been chanting Hurricane's name in the streets all morning.

The general view was, with the team losing so badly and Otis Campbell and his hapless players making so many mistakes, that the West Indies had only one chance – to get this kid Hurricane Hamish out there in a maroon cap playing for his country. The crowd in the courthouse, the whole island of Jamaica and indeed all of the West Indies people spoke with one voice about that (excluding Rough, Otis and, of course, Rich Vermin, who had again taken his seat tucked away in a back corner of the room where no one could see him).

Moreover, apart from the three villains, the whole of the Caribbean had also been deeply touched by the personal story of Hurricane

Hamish. They had been moved by the words of Wesley Clarke, FT and Hurricane in the court-house ten days before, words which had been faithfully reported by the secret correspondent in *The Caribbean Chronicle*. No one could see why Hurricane should not stay with the old man. Anything else seemed like mere cruelty for the sake of the pride of the law.

There was a buzz of anticipation as Judge Herring swept in, adopting his usual theatrical style. He smelt that atmosphere again in the court today – as if the minds of the people in front of him were speaking to him. The people were involved in a way that he had not known in any of the other cases he had tried over the years. The Jamaican people really cared about this kid.

He sat and surveyed the courthouse, *his* courthouse as he always thought of it. He stroked his white beard thoughtfully. His eyes were drawn to the boy. Judge Herring was a great cricket fan himself. He was doubtful, looking at this lanky kid who seemed so young, that he could really be as good or as fast as everybody said he was. But then he looked at the sea of faces and realized that the people clearly thought so. They were here to see Hurricane free to be a true West Indian, free to play calypso cricket. They were in no mood for any other sort of decision from the judge – he was fully aware of that.

He signalled with his hand for everyone to sit

down, and except for those squeezed in and standing up in the gallery they dropped as one into their wooden benches and chairs.

Hurricane was fidgety. He felt extremely nervous. He knew that today the judge was going to ask him very awkward questions about his life with FT at Treasure Beach and he was worried about saying the wrong thing. He looked over his shoulder up to the gallery for the mystery girl. He hoped again for the strength he had mustered in her presence before, but he searched the sea of faces in vain. She was nowhere to be seen.

The attendant spoke to the judge and turned to the court and called Hurricane Hamish to the stand.

"Just tell the truth," FT had said to him. "Just tell things as they are and we should be OK."

However, Hurricane was fretful as he held the Bible and took the oath. His hand shook and the holy book's pages flapped around. He looked helplessly at the mass of people watching him.

The judge was asking him a question.

"So you go out fishing all alone, young man?"

Hurricane turned his eyes from the people in the courthouse to Judge Herring.

"What? Oh sure," he said reluctantly. "I know the sea better than our back yard. I've been out on my own in the boat since I was ten years old."

As he spoke, he felt he was saying the wrong things. It was not like the last time, when the mystery girl had been there. He knew he was getting it all badly wrong.

"There's no safety issue then?" said the judge. "Can't the waters around the Pedro Banks be very dangerous?"

"Well. They can be," said Hurricane tentatively. "I know what I'm doing though. I grew up with them."

Judge Herring was writing again. That always made Hurricane nervous.

"You have never been to school, I hear?" continued the judge, stroking his beard as he quizzed the boy.

"FT taught me," said Hurricane. "He gave me all my lessons. Like he told you ten days ago when he was standing up here. I'm better than most of the kids in the school. I learnt to read from FT's library of cricket books."

The judge frowned.

"If you don't go to school, young man, what plans have you got for a career?"

"I beg your pardon, sir?"

"A job!" said Judge Herring impatiently.

The court caught its breath.

Again Hurricane looked desperately up into the gallery. The mystery girl was there – standing at the back, squeezed in between two old women. She had arrived at last. What had kept her?

Hurricane smiled – that sense of assurance was with him again.

"That's the easiest question you asked me so far, sir."

The judge noticed a new confidence and strength in Hurricane's voice.

"Well?" Herring said.

"I'm going to play cricket for the West Indies. That's if you will let me. Seems to me like it's up to you whether I get a decent job or not, Judge Herring, sir. It seems a bit weird to bug me about it, when you've got the power to make sure I have the chance to do what I really want. I just want to be a fast bowler and win Test matches for my country."

There was a hush. People waited for Herring's reaction to Hurricane's cheek. Then someone right up in the back of the gallery started applauding, a slow solitary clap at first. Some others joined in and the applause swept like a wave across the courthouse. The people rose to their feet and they were clapping and shouting and cheering – calling for common sense and compassion from the judge.

Judge Herring was furious. He hammered on his wooden block with the large mallet he kept by his right hand, but his banging was drowned by the noise. Only when the noise subsided and the people were silent could he be heard.

"If there is a commotion like that one more time, I will have this courthouse evacuated and we will conduct this case behind closed doors. Now be quiet! All of you! I won't have such a rabble in my court!"

He scowled at the faces before him.

Hurricane stood nervously in the box. He felt the judge's anger was a very bad sign. It troubled him greatly.

There was calm at last in the court, but at this moment the huge doors swung open and a policeman entered the courthouse. It was the big, burly policeman who stood outside the building and guarded the entrance. He came purposefully forward to the bench. The court watched him walk up the aisle, his huge black boots seeming to echo an ominous warning around the courthouse. Judge Herring was cross at another interruption, but the fixed look on the policeman's face indicated that it was serious. He approached the judge and leant over to whisper to him.

From where he stood close to the judge, Hurricane could pick out a few of the words which passed between them: "certificate ... parents ... England ... towel ... here ... outside ... now..."

Judge Herring was nodding, and a concentrated and serious look came over him.

Hurricane heard him speak to the big policeman.

"Go and bring them in, then."

The policeman strode purposefully back out of the door. Soon he returned. Behind him walked a man and a woman. They were a nice-looking couple, dressed smartly and with a certain amount of poise. They were both smiling warmly and particularly looking at Hurricane with a great deal of affection. All eyes in the courthouse followed them as they walked towards Hurricane and Judge Herring. Nobody knew, of course, that they were Rich Vermin's agents. At the back of the court Rich had to contain himself from laughing by chewing a huge piece of treacle toffee.

The couple followed the policeman all the way to the bench and stood before Judge Herring. The woman looked in a motherly sort of way at Hurricane. Rich Vermin was the only one in the courtroom smiling. The rest of the court was bewildered by yet another twist in this drama.

The man had handed Judge Herring a file of papers, including a certificate. It was the birth certificate Rich had given them, claiming Hurricane as their son. The woman handed Judge Herring an MCC towel.

"We used to have another towel like this," she said. "I wrapped the boy in it when he was tiny, the day he disappeared."

Judge Herring read the certificate and was comparing the towel with Exhibit A. The certificate looked quite genuine and the towels made a perfectly matching pair.

As Herring was studying them, the man held out his arms and approached Hurricane.

"My son! My son!" he called out.

The woman followed his actions.

"Our boy! Our boy!" she shouted.

The whole court gasped. Some people stood up to see better what was going on. People started talking. Someone was shouting. All hell had broken loose in the courtroom. Judge Herring was banging his mallet. Hurricane pushed away the arms of the man and stared hopelessly up at the gallery. The mystery girl was the only one who looked calm.

If only someone could do something to help him prove all this was wrong, thought Hurricane. These people were phoney. Something deep inside him knew that for sure.

Judge Herring stood up. He was still hammering away like mad on the wooden block. The policeman had joined him in trying to silence the hullabaloo and was blowing his whistle. Eventually the court started to hush, a silence descended and the racket drained away. Judge Herring signalled everyone to sit down. He indicated the couple should stand to the side of the court. He held up the piece of paper he had in his hand.

"This – people of Jamaica – is an English birth certificate. It confirms that a child was born to this couple twelve years and nine months ago."

A shudder of astonishment went through everyone watching – everyone except Rich Vermin, who again had to suppress a giggle.

"These people are called Jones. Mister Jones is a member of the MCC. The towel he has brought exactly matches the one Hurricane Hamish was found in as a baby. With the birth certificate are some police reports from England. They confirm and verify the following:

"Mrs Jones used to swaddle the child in an MCC towel. Days after its birth the child disappeared from their home in England and was never re-discovered. These papers claim to offer the proof that Hurricane Hamish is in fact a boy called John Jones, and that..."

"No they don't! Stop that now! These people are frauds!"

Somebody was shouting. Everyone in the court turned towards the big wooden doors at the back where the sound came from.

The voice came from the now open doorway at the back of the courthouse. Judge Herring swallowed his words in astonishment. Standing there was a tall man with glasses. Everyone recognized him. It was Harry Hack, the editor of *The Caribbean Chronicle*.

Hurricane watched as the editor, with a deter-mined look of intent on his face, approached the bench. He carried what looked like a tape recorder in one hand and a tiny object in the other.

"Explain this interruption, Mister Hack!" Judge Herring shouted at the editor.

"It explains itself," Harry Hack said. "Or this will."

He held up a small cassette.

"It's a tape. It was collected and sent to me by

the secret correspondent of our newspaper. Allow me to play it for you."

He set the tape recorder down in front of Judge Herring, slipped the tape in and pressed the *play* button. The buzz around the court fell to a hush as the words started. The editor turned and smiled at Hurricane.

The tape played. The voices of the Jones couple and one other voice were clearly heard.

"...Have you got that then?..."

"...We enter the courthouse as he is questioning the boy..."

"...yes... And you give him the fake certificate..."

"...Here it is..."

"...very impressive. This should fool everyone..."

"...other papers too..."

"...all that made-up stuff about the MCC towel..."

"...pretend to be emotional. Hug the boy or some-thing..."

"...they'll really think he's ours... I love it..."

"...this should make up Herring's mind for him..."

"...and keep the boy out of the West Indies team..."

"...OK. We've got the picture. Now let's see the money..."

As the tape clicked dead, everyone – not for the first time that day – held their breath.

"Arrest these people," said the judge to the huge policeman.

The policeman moved quickly and grabbed an arm of each of them. The couple were too startled and dumbstruck to react at all and were led away and out of the courthouse. Moments before, Rich Vermin had slipped away unnoticed through the doors at the back of the court. Everyone was talking – noise filled the place. Hurricane just stood there with a huge grin on his face.

"Now settle down," said Judge Herring.

The court gradually calmed itself.

The judge turned and spoke to Hurricane. The court hung on his every word.

Judge Herring made his pronouncement.

"Young man. It is clear to me that your origins remain unknown. As the man you call FT –" he moved his head to indicate the old man on the front row – "as the man you call FT says, you seem to have been brought in on the wind. The adoption procedure performed by Treasure Beach chief of police Wesley Clarke was both illegal and irregular.

"There is also evidence of what we might call unconventionality in your upbringing. The evidence of this case appears, astonishingly, to indicate that you are only twelve years old, yet you do not attend school and you fish the Pedro Banks alone and have done since the age of ten. However..."

Judge Herring paused, the court still hanging on his every word.

"...Officer Clarke appears to have acted outside the law, but nevertheless in good faith. His intentions were sound. He made a moral decision. That decision appears to have worked.

"I do not wish to encourage such practices and the law takes a dim view of them, but in this case they appear the understandable actions of an honourable man.

"Your upbringing, though unconventional, appears to have been a loving one. Indeed in some ways it could hardly have been better. There is no precedent for this case, but, since I have no desire to separate you from your guardian, I shall, indeed, grant the papers to legalize the adoption."

There were murmurs of approval and a spattering of applause around the courthouse, but Judge Herring held up his hand to silence the people.

"This brings me to the matter of your citizenship and nationality. There is no legitimate claim on you from elsewhere – despite these bizarre and deceitful antics in this court today. Strictly, your origins remain unknown."

The judge smiled briefly.

"Perhaps you *were* just blown in on the wind," he chuckled. "With your adoption papers, I thereby grant you full identity and nationality papers making you a Jamaican. You are free to all such associated rights. You are free – even – if the selectors deem that it should ever be so, to play cricket for the West Indies."

Judge Herring smiled. He held up his hand again to silence the noises of approval coming from all sides.

"In fact," he said, "may I be the first to wish you good luck in the third Test. The secret correspondent's articles must have been right all along. I think it is your destiny to play in the rest of the series and to try and turn it around for us."

Hurricane broke into his grin. FT and Wesley were hugging each other. Harry Hack was shaking Judge Herring's hand.

Judge Herring handed Hurricane one of the MCC towels. It was Exhibit A – the towel he had been found in all those years ago. He gave the matching one to Harry Hack.

"Take these as souvenirs," he said to them.

Harry Hack smiled.

"I know what I'll do," he said. "I'll make sure this one gets to the secret correspondent. As a thank you from us all."

Hurricane nodded his approval and took his towel gratefully from Judge Herring.

Judge Herring turned to the rows of people.

"This hearing is closed," he shouted, banging his mallet on the wooden block.

Hurricane was virtually mobbed as the courtroom erupted and hats and caps and books and newspapers were thrown into the air.

10

Cartwheels of Joy

Third Test at The Antigua Recreation Ground, St John's, Antigua

First Day

Judge Herring had read the mood of the people and the selectors correctly. Drastic remedies were required to kick-start the West Indies team back into this series and Hurricane was the man – or boy – who everyone was hoping would provide the impetus. Two-nil down and three to play represented a big mountain to climb.

The West Indies manager Brian Lara stood on the dressing-room balcony with Hurricane Hamish and surveyed the scene at The Antigua Recreation Ground. Hurricane looked over at his manager and there was a misty faraway look in the little man's eyes. Lara loved it here. It had been the scene of his historic and record breaking 375 against England, all those years ago back in 1994.

On the opposition balcony stood Michael Atherton – Lara's counterpart as England manager. He had been the England captain for that match in 1994. He knew a lot about Lara, and, when they had been players, he had spent rather more time than he would have liked watching him bat. He looked over to the West Indies balcony and waved to him. Lara waved back. For his part, he had seen Atherton make a fair few runs against the West Indies, too.

Atherton knew less, however, about the kid and new cap Lara was talking to. Atherton rubbed his face, pondering. The England camp were a little concerned. They had heard a lot about the child Hurricane and they were all aware of the extraordinary drama of the court case over in Jamaica. None of the English players or management, however, had ever seen him bowl. They had no videos of him, nothing at all. Nevertheless, on this track Atherton still felt they should bat if they won the toss.

West Indies had Hurricane Hamish in for Padmore, but had kept faith with Charlie Constantine. He had just been preferred to Radwick Scorpio. The selectors had debated the inexplicable blindness problems a lot of the players had complained of at Trinidad and had decided to keep faith with their batsmen.

This was definitely a vital match for Charlie's Test future, through no fault of his own. The illness in the first Test and the flashing light in the second remained a mystery.

England had brought in Bill Collins for Ferrers, who had had a mediocre tour so far, and preferred Wentworth to Tilney, wanting the extra seamer rather than the second spinner.

Hurricane looked out over the ground. The two captains were out there and a TV crew was recording the toss.

"Do you fancy a bowl this morning?" asked Lara.

"I really do," said Hurricane, with a huge, but somewhat strained smile. "I don't want to spend time in the dressing-room getting nervous while we're batting."

"I've got a feeling we'll be bowling," said Lara. "They will want to bat – it has worked for them in the first two Tests and this is a good wicket – but we want to set you against Smith as early as we can, in any case. We want to really take the fight to them."

"Sure," said Hurricane, nodding nervously.

At that moment Fitzwilliam Darcy did a batting motion up towards Mike Atherton who raised a hand in acknowledgement and went inside to start preparing his opening batsmen. England had won the toss and chosen to bat.

Lara patted Hurricane on the back.

"Go and get warmed up with Fish," he said.

Otis Campbell led out the West Indies team to warm applause from a packed Antiguan crowd. A man in a yellow suit danced some cartwheels on the outfield as the players came out. Whistles blew and reggae pumped out from a huge boom box stereo across the ground. Hurricane ran ahead of the others, galloping out on to the parched outfield with his huge strides and his bare feet. He stopped and looked around the ground and the people were cheering him, celebrating the début they had all been waiting too long for. He raised an arm in embarrassed acknowledgement. Fish ran over to him.

"Get your mind on the game, Hurricane. You and I have got work to do."

Charlie Constantine came to have a word with him. Hurricane was pleased Charlie was in the team.

"Remember, Hurricane," said Charlie. "Give it everything you've got. Be fast."

Hurricane smiled, but his stomach was churning.

There was some polite applause for the England openers, Smith and Martin. Smith strode purposefully to the far end. He was to take guard for the first over from Fish Archibald. Hurricane was sent by Otis to field down at long leg. Otis was still annoyed that Hurricane was in the side – but how could he stand up to the opinion of all the other selectors and just about every cricket fan in the West Indies?

It was a good and probing first over from Fish. Inevitably Smith flailed away – trying as always for some early boundaries – but he slashed them along the ground straight to fielders and missed a couple which left him in the air. The last ball of the over Fish dug in short. Smith hooked but played too early and the ball bounced off his glove along the ground down to Hurricane at long leg. The two English batsmen trotted the single.

So Hurricane's first ball in Test cricket would be to Smithy the Slogger. Smith had been a great success in this series in the start to his own Test career, with scores so far of 214, 55 and 34, at an average of 101. He and fast bowler Willoughby had been the real heroes for England in the first two Tests.

As Hurricane walked from long leg to begin the next over, the crowd started a handclap of anticipation. They started slowly, then began to clap faster and faster. As Hurricane marked out his run there was crescendo of noise from the people. They had seen their team lose two humiliating Test matches while this kid had been in court and banned. Now his moment had come.

Smith twirled his bat and then tapped with it at his popping crease. He watched Hurricane start to charge in and heard the clapping and roaring of the local crowd. He had one thing on his mind. To give this first ball one big thump, and with it to take a big swipe at Hurricane's confidence.

As he raced in, Hurricane's mind was busy, too. Be fast, be fast, be fast.

He let go and the ball was fast and short, just on off stump. Smith was on to the back foot and across in a flash and he caught it full in the meat of the bat as he hooked at it. The ball flew miles in the air and disappeared over mid-wicket for six.

Second Day

FT sat with Hurricane in his hotel room, contemplating the previous day's play together. England were an astonishing 330 for 2. Smith, already with his second sparkling century of the series to his name, had slept soundly on 175 not out. Hurricane had slept less well on figures of 20-0-85-0. It was hardly the start to Test match cricket he had dreamt of. As things got worse and worse through the day he had searched the faces in the crowd desperately for the mystery girl, but in vain. The day had been one big nightmare.

"Things will be different today," said FT.

Hurricane shook his head. He felt tired after yesterday. Why had Otis bowled him at Smith for so long when the batsman was clearly on top? Why hadn't the captain used him in shorter spells to keep him fresh, especially when he was bowling waywardly? Above all, though, how was he going to find some rhythm and some accuracy today?

"Stop worrying," said FT. "You started badly that time you bowled to Charlie in the nets – and in the Jamaica versus Trinidad game."

"I didn't bowl badly for a whole day, though,"

groaned Hurricane. "Maybe I'm not good enough after all, like that Rough Tungsten says in the paper today."

Hurricane had just read Rough's morning article in *The West Indies Wayfarer*. His headline had said it all: *HURRICANE BLOWS HIMSELF OUT.*

"Keep your head up," said FT. "Today is another day."

Hurricane nodded, but he felt nervous and a bit sick inside.

"And remember," said FT. "Be fast."

Otis Campbell had no words for Hurricane the next morning, which, from the captain supposed to be getting the best out of him, was a surprise. However, Fish and Charlie took him to one side. They encouraged him to keep his confidence and not be afraid to be fast. Just like good old FT had said.

As the team walked out, Hurricane decided to come out last to try to change his luck. From that day onwards he would always walk out last in every Test match he ever played in.

He was about to enter the field of play, when a voice called out from behind him. He turned to look. Up in the back of the pavilion a girl stood waving. Hurricane immediately recognized the mystery girl. He waved back at her and ran out on to the ground with a new spring in his step. The excited fan – in a green suit today – did cartwheels on the outfield.

Otis came up to Hurricane: "Have an early crack at Smith, will you?" he said, handing Hurricane the ball.

Otis was smiling to himself. The boy's disaster yesterday was a real bonus. Another bad day today and the series – and this child's confidence – should be well and truly lost. Rich Vermin would be happy and he and Rough could bank their money. The plan to lose this series had worked beautifully.

As he stood at the end of his run and the squat figure of Smith faced him, Hurricane felt a surge of strength flow through his veins and throughout his whole body. He felt inside him that his moment had come, at last. He willed himself to be fast.

He ran in, gliding with his enormous barefooted strides like a huge thoroughbred racehorse over the turf. As he reached the stumps he let go of a ball which seemed to zip through the air like a firecracker. It jumped off a length at Smith's throat, flicked his glove as he flung up his hand to protect himself and went through to Andy Alleyne. The whole West Indies side went up for the catch and Umpire Adams raised the finger. Smith was out. England 330 for 3. The crowd had gone crazy with delight and that man in the green suit was on the outfield again, cavorting and cart-wheeling in front of the stand.

Knightley came to the wicket, took guard and surveyed the field. Hurricane eyed him from the end of his run. He felt full of power – strength seeping through every nerve and sinew in his body. He glided in again. This ball was full and swung in late and viciously. Knightley hardly saw it before his leg stump was cartwheeling around and dancing a jig behind him. England 330 for 4. Hurricane Hamish was on a hat-trick. The crowd was going bananas. This was the calypso cricket they had been waiting for.

Darcy was the next man in for England – their experienced skipper and all-rounder. Hurricane eyed him, and the batsman fiddled nervously with his thigh pad.

Hurricane ran in again – if anything faster yet more gracefully than for the previous two balls. This one was just short of a length and hit the seam and moved away from Darcy. It beat the outside edge and flew through to Alleyne. The crowd groaned in disappointment at the missed hat-trick, but then a huge wall of noise of applause and whistles and drums went over the ground, as the crowd rewarded Hurricane's effort, urging him on for more wickets.

"Be fast! You can do it! Be fast!"

The crowd did not have long to wait for more celebration. The next ball was even faster. It took the top of Darcy's outside edge and flew like a bullet high to first slip. Charlie Constantine – in the reflex action more of a teenager than a man of his age – flung up his left hand. The ball fizzed right into it and stuck. England 330 for 5 – three wickets in four balls on his Test début for Hurricane. All the players – with the exception of Otis, who almost seemed to be sneering – ran as one to hug him. The crowd went absolutely berserk and the man in the green suit cartwheeled and cartwheeled and cartwheeled for joy!

The collapse continued. Hurricane picked up two more wickets to finish with 5 for 105 while Fish chipped in with two wickets and Larry King with one. England had succumbed sensationally and were all out for 395. They had lost eight wickets for 65 runs in just over an hour and a half.

Despite the intense pressure he was under, the rest of the day belonged to Charlie Constantine. Otis went quickly, deliberately playing round a straight one from Wickham, but Charlie had good partnerships with Matthews and James and at the close West Indies were 205 for 2 – right back in the match, with Charlie 99 not out overnight, having batted beautifully, just like his old self.

It had been a sensational day's cricket and the West Indies first successful day of the series. People were starting to believe they could win this match.

Third Day

When a loosener from Darcy was steered past cover and a single was run off the first ball of the morning, Hurricane Hamish stood with the whole of the West Indies team and management on the dressing-room balcony to acclaim Charlie Constantine's twenty fifth Test match century – his seventh against England.

Charlie had not finished, though. After the buzz had died down, he took guard once again and settled in to bat carefully and sensibly all day long for another century. He passed 200 in the last over of the day and the cartwheeling fan – wearing a peach suit today – flipped and somersaulted around the outfield in joyous celebration.

Charlie had held the West Indies batting together all day, with useful support from Alleyne and late on from Archibald. By the close the West Indies had reached 431 for 8 – a lead of 36, and with a slight upper hand in the match. Only Hurricane was left to come in.

Rough Tungsten rolled over in bed, woken from his dream by the impertinent ringing of the phone. Only one person would ring him at this time of night – it was three in the morning.

"Uh?" he grunted into the receiver, rubbing his eyes.

"What's going on?"

Rich Vermin was virtually screaming down the phone.

"Hello Rich," croaked Rough wearily. "How are you?"

"Is that all you can say, man? What are you going to do about this?"

Here we go again, thought Rough.

"Not much I can do, Rich. We agreed to let this match go its own course. How were we to know Constantine would find all his old magic?"

There was snorting from the other end of the line.

"If England win this one, you two idiots will have me to answer to."

After what seemed to be the noise of some banging, as if Rich was hitting his receiver against a wall, the line went dead.

Rough put down the receiver and rolled over, groaning. Without the devil's potion or the magic mirrors, and with Hurricane bowling well and Constantine back in the runs, things were rather spiralling out of control.

Fourth Day

Frankie Genus was out early the next day and the adoring West Indies public had their first, very brief exposure to the comical and useless batting of Hurricane Hamish. Hurricane strode to the wicket with his long strides, but with a bat in his hands and boots on his feet he looked lanky and awkward and clumsy. Charlie came down to speak to him.

"Just try and get some bat on it, and I'm ready for the quick single," he said, and he gave Hurricane an encouraging pat on the side.

Hurricane had hardly ever got a bat on anything in his life and today was to be no exception. He did not even look as though he knew how he should be holding the bat. Wickham ran in and bowled a fairly innocuous and straight delivery. Hurricane swung and missed and the ball clipped the top of his off stump. It was his first – but probably not his last – golden duck in Test cricket. West Indies were all out for 435 – a first innings lead of 40.

Fish and Hurricane started well with two early wickets apiece and at lunch England had slumped to 70 for 4. Most importantly, Fish trapped Smith lbw with one which cut back a long way off the seam. Mysteriously though (except to himself, to Rough Tungsten watching from the press box and to Rich Vermin sitting up in the stands), Otis Campbell continued with the spinners King and Genus after lunch, giving each of them a long spell on a pitch which had been favouring the quicker bowlers and showing little turn. Knightley and Darcy got going and looked good for England and the afternoon session brought them a gritty but valuable 75 runs. They lost no wickets, to be 145 for 4 and 105 ahead at tea.

Lara and Richards gave Otis a serious lecture

during the interval and, after their telling him to use the quicker bowlers, he was forced to bowl Hurricane, Fish and Roy Amory for the rest of the day. The three of them did a good job with a wicket each. At the close England were 207 for 7, only 167 ahead, with three wickets left and just a day left to play.

Fifth Day
England had no chance to win the match, but they could draw if they batted for as long as possible. Early wickets were vital for the West Indies, if they were going to give themselves time to chase the total and win. England batted doggedly, Campbell did not use his bowlers as well as he might have done and it took the whole of the morning session to winkle out the last three wickets. Inexplicably to the crowd, Otis set some overly-defensive fields and some edges went into gaps around the bat where fielders might have been. Finally Fish had the last man, Willoughby, given out lbw just before the interval.

In this time England had added a very cagey 45 – leaving the West Indies two sessions to make 213 and get back in the series. This would mean getting a move on if they were going to have any chance to make the runs in the limited amount of time available.

Charlie Constantine opened the batting after lunch

with Otis Campbell. Charlie was into his stride immediately. He continued his form from the first innings – seeing it like a football and middling everything. What the crowd found strange was that Otis – normally a naturally attacking player – got very bogged down, and at times did not even seem to be trying to score quickly. After an hour the West Indies were only 35 for 0, their chances of making the runs receding.

In desperation Charlie went down the wicket to have a word with his captain.

"We've got to get a move on, skipper. We can win this if we accelerate. Play a few shots."

Otis Campbell sneered at him.

"You trying to tell me how to bat now, Constantine?"

"No, but we can win, if..."

"Just remember who the captain is around here," spat Otis.

Otis turned his back on him and went to face the next ball from Willoughby. He never knew it, but with that next delivery Willoughby won the game for the West Indies. He held this one back a bit and, prodding forward, Otis played a little too early and offered the bowler a return catch. 35 for 1.

Charlie need not have worried now. He played beautifully himself and both Matthews and James were on top form, making a very brisk 43 and 50 respectively. England flagged in the heat and their bowling became ragged.

Eventually the West Indies cruised home to win by six wickets. Charlie made 106 not out – and got the Man of the Match award for a double century and a century, both not out, in the same game.

On another good note, Hurricane Hamish had arrived with a début of huge impact. On a bad note, the questions were humming amongst the fans about the captaincy and the peculiar batting of Otis Campbell.

Long after the other fans had gone home a man in a bright red suit was turning cartwheels of joy on the outfield celebrating a West Indies win – still two-one down but certainly back in the series.

The four of them were sitting there waiting for him – Richards, Lara, Ambrose and Walsh. Otis sneered at them. So it had come to this. What a mess. Why had he ever got involved with Rich Vermin and Rough Tungsten? And why had fate sent along this kid Hurricane Hamish – to make any plan to make England lose seem impossible?

The fates were cruel, so cruel. He could have retired as a national hero, but instead, because of becoming one of the three villains and all the cheating and deceit, everyone was calling for his head. He knew that the selectors had no choice really. They had to sack him as captain – but he was going to walk away from it all before they could.

He had the worst of all worlds. He would never get his money for the farm from Vermin and he'd lost his treasured job as West Indies captain. Oh why had he ever got into this? A sad and lonely retirement beckoned.

He sat down wearily at the end of the table.

"You know why we've called you here, don't you?" said Viv Richards.

"Yeah. To congratulate me on pulling us back to only two-one down in the series," said Otis sarcastically.

"I think we all know we won this one despite you, not because of you," said Ambrose. "Thanks to Charlie – and Fish and Hurricane."

Otis sneered again, curling his lip and drawing his breath in a bitter snort of disdain.

"I'm not going to sit here and take this from you goons," he said.

The four men shook their heads. This from the captain they had appointed. This tirade of abuse to men who only had the good of West Indies cricket at heart.

"Otis, please," said Viv Richards. "We're as upset as you. Can you not tell us what has happened? What is it that has changed you from such a shrewd captain into such an erratic one? And why were you batting so slowly when we needed quick runs to get the win?"

Otis laughed. If only he could tell them. If only he could come clean. If only he could admit everything

– about the devil's potion, the magic mirrors, about Rich Vermin and Rough Tungsten. But that was impossible now.

He pushed his chair back and stood up abruptly. This was it then – the end of the road, the end of his career. It crossed his mind that Charlie Constantine would get his job. That hurt a lot.

He spat out the final words.

"You can have your useless job. I quit. I'm not playing for you lot again."

He headed quickly for the door and slammed it violently on his way out.

Viv Richards looked at the others. They were all equally shocked.

"Oh well," he said. "No point crying over spilt milk. We've got two Test matches to win in Barbados and Jamaica. I think we should appoint Charlie Constantine as skipper for the rest of the series right now. And we'll bring in Radwick Scorpio to open instead of Otis. Everyone agree?"

The three other men nodded as one. It was the only choice.

"I'll go and get Charlie," said Lara, getting up from his chair.

Rough Tungsten bumped into Otis outside the ground. Otis was quickly getting into his car and seemed to be hurrying away.

"Hey, Otis!" Rough called after him as he climbed into his BMW.

Rough ran towards the car, flailing his arms in panic. Otis scowled but opened the window.

"I'm off," he growled. "You're on your own with Rich Vermin now."

Rough Tungsten's heart sank.

"You can't..."

Otis sneered.

"Just watch me. I'm off, I told you. That's it."

"You can't, Otis... Where are you going?"

"South America. You won't hear from me again."

Rough Tungsten was panicking.

"But, Rich said..."

Otis cut off his words with a wave of his hand.

"I don't care. He's ruined my career and my reputation. You're welcome to him. And the two of you can cheat as much as you like, but you won't stop Hurricane Hamish. Goodbye for ever."

Otis gave one last sneer at Rough and the window rose between them. The car sped off, skidding on the gravel and showering Rough Tungsten with stones and pebbles.

THIRD TEST SCORECARD

England

	1st Innings			2nd Innings		
S T L Smith	c Alleyne	b Hamish	175	lbw	b Archibald	17
R Martin	c Amory	b Genus	54	c Alleyne	b Hamish	6
W T Collins	c Campbell	b Genus	44	c Constantine	b Archibald	26
C P Bingley		b King	53	c Amory	b Hamish	10
G Knightley		b Hamish	0	lbw	b Amory	53
F W Darcy*	c Constantine	b Hamish	0	c Constantine	b Hamish	65
E L Bertram	c Alleyne	b Archibald	21	c Alleyne	b Archibald	1
F S Churchill+	c Goldman	b Hamish	9	c Genus	b Hamish	11
F R Wentworth	lbw	b Hamish	9		b Amory	18
G D Wickham	lbw	b Archibald	0		not out	21
J Willoughby		not out	7	lbw	b Archibald	11
Extras	(b10, lb5, nb8)		23	(b2, lb6, nb5)		13

Total	**(all out)**	**395**	**(all out)**	**252**

Fall of Wickets 1-134,2-261,3-330,4-330,5-330,   1-14,2-30,3-47,4-68,5-175,
6-358,7-368,8-372,9-383,10-395   6-178,7-204,8-221,9-237,10-252

Bowling	O	M	R	W	O	M	R	W
F S Archibald	29	6	82	2	29	5	67	4
H Hamish	31	3	105	5	22	3	51	4
R P B Amory	17	0	63	0	25	2	63	2
L V A King	22	2	66	1	20	6	32	0
F R Genus	12	0	64	2	19	2	31	0

West Indies

	1st Innings			2nd Innings		
C Constantine		not out	204		not out	106
O K Campbell*		b Wickham	12		c & b Willoughby	5
R P Matthews	c Bertram	b Darcy	41		run out	43
J J James	c Knightley	b Willoughby	47	c Churchill	b Wentworth	50
B Goldman	lbw	b Bertram	2	lbw	b Bertram	7
A C Alleyne+		b Wentworth	80		not out	0
L V A King	c Martin	b Wentworth	8			
R P B Amory	c Churchill	b Wickham	3			
F S Archibald	c Collins	b Darcy	18			
F R Genus		b Willoughby	0			
H Hamish		b Wickham	0			
Extras	(b4, lb7, nb7, w2)		20	(lb2, nb2)		4

Total	**(all out)**	**435**	**(for 4 wickets)**	**215**

Fall of Wickets 1-30,2-128,3-225,4-230,5-377,   1-35,2-104,3-190,4-211
6-390,7-393,8-431,9-435,10-435

Bowling	O	M	R	W	O	M	R	W
J Willoughby	35	4	111	2	12	0	50	1
G D Wickham	29	5	71	3	14	0	58	0
F R Wentworth	29	4	84	2	9	0	43	1
E L Bertram	39	7	102	1	10	3	34	1
F W Darcy	23	6	56	2	10	2	28	0

Man of the Match: C Constantine (West Indies)
West Indies won by 6 wickets

11

The Mystery Girl

Treasure Beach, Jamaica

Hurricane sat on the sand and looked out over the Caribbean Sea. It was late in the evening and the waves had calmed, leaving the aquamarine-coloured water as calm as a lake, almost like a glass surface with barely a ripple. He was pre-occupied, thinking about the beautiful mystery girl.

He could see her face in his mind's eye and he wondered who she was and where she came from. Who was the mystery girl?

He had seen her several times now. At Black River that day, when she had made him want to do so well and unbeknown to him, Charlie Constantine had been there. That had been the start of it all. Then she had been at Sabina Park for the trial, sitting up there in the stand. Then at the Jamaica versus Trinidad game he had only started to bowl well when he had miraculously seen her in the crowd. Then in court, just her being there had seemed to help him to speak up for himself in front of all those people. Then at the Test match – he had bowled awfully on the first day when she seemed not to be around, then had seen her in the pavilion at the start of the second day, and from that point he had felt like the best bowler who ever walked on to a cricket ground in a West Indies cap.

Who was she? He had to find her. That was the most important thing now.

He went back along the beach to the house and found FT frying some fish, whistling a reggae rhythm through his teeth. The old man was happy. The West Indies were back to winning ways and his boy had opened his account in Test cricket with a dramatic performance and figures of 5 for 105 and 4 for 51. Shame about the golden duck – but he'd never seen Hurricane make a run in any case. The world could not be sweeter.

He looked up at Hurricane as the boy came in.

"Hi, Hurricane. Cuttlefish suit you OK today?"

"Sure," said Hurricane, sitting down wearily into a chair.

FT looked at the boy.

"What's the matter with you? You don't look like a new cricket hero to me. You look more like something is troubling you."

Hurricane managed a feeble smile.

"FT?"

"What, son?"

The fish sizzled in the olive oil and garlic and FT drew in the lovely aromas. Hurricane chewed his lip, uncertain how to put this.

"Well?" said FT.

"How would you go about finding someone, if say you had no idea of their name or who they were but you just kept spotting them and they kept disappearing?"

FT paused, holding his fork over the griddle.

"I guess you just have to wait until that person came to you, in that case."

Hurricane sighed, impatiently.

"But what if you liked having them around?"

FT stood still again. The skin of the fish was browning nicely.

"What's all this about, Hurricane?"

Hurricane drummed the table with his fingers. How could he get FT's advice without telling him everything? He knew the old fellow would tease him if he talked about the girl.

"It's a friend of mine," he said. "He keeps seeing someone who he needs to meet properly. Someone he has to track down."

"Which friend?" said FT. He turned the fish over.

"Oh. That's not important."

Hurricane could not see the mild smile on FT's face.

"Well," said FT. "I think you should tell your friend to be patient and to trust to time and chance to bring him the meeting he's looking for."

Hurricane groaned.

"I thought you might say something like that," he said.

He looked very fed up. Still, the fish turned out well. FT had cooked it to his usual perfection and he served it up for Hurricane with a massive helping of rice and peas. The old man might not be able to help him find the mystery girl but he could cook fish all right.

After dinner – and they had eaten fairly early so it was still light – Hurricane took a walk up to the police station. He knew Wesley was there, reinstated and back in uniform. He surely would have some ideas about how to track someone down. He was a policeman after all.

Hurricane found him asleep – Wesley in his familiar pose, snoring at his desk. He would never learn, thought Hurricane, with affection towards the man to whom he owed so much.

It had caused him enough trouble already when Hurricane's secret file had been stolen, but come the end of the day and the setting sun Wesley just could not resist popping his feet up on the desk and taking that glorious nap. At least there were big padlocks on the filing cabinet now.

Hurricane coughed. Wesley stirred and spoke in his dream: "Put Fish Archibald on."

"Put Hurricane Hamish on, you mean," called out Hurricane, beaming a grin as Wesley shuddered and flung his head up in shock as he jerked awake.

"Oh, Hurricane, it's only you," he said, with relief.

"Only me," Hurricane laughed. "I could have been off into the sunset with a file from your cabinet," he said, teasing the man.

Wesley's face clouded.

"I don't want to go through all that again. Thank goodness for those new locks. Anyway, what brings you up here? You must be after something."

Hurricane laughed.

"I suppose I am. I want the advice of the newly reinstated chief of police for Treasure Beach," he said, flashing another huge grin at Wesley.

"Advice," the policeman said. "Well, I'm flattered. You must be looking for some advice on how to bowl a decent slower ball. Now, I was watching you on the TV for the Antigua Test and there were times when I wanted you to just slip in the slower one, you know, mix it up a bit, keep those English guessing, and then, after that..."

"WESLEY!" shouted Hurricane.

"What?" said the officer.

"It's not advice on my bowling I need. You really think I would come to you for that when I share a dressing-room with Fish Archibald and the selectors include Curtly Ambrose and Courtney Walsh?"

Wesley looked hurt.

"This is something much more important," said Hurricane quickly.

"Oh," said Wesley, brightening up. "Well, fire away then."

Hurricane took a deep breath.

"I need to find someone. Someone I keep seeing around."

"Who?" asked Wesley, intrigued.

"Well, that's the point," said Hurricane wearily. "I'm not at all sure who it is."

"All sounds very mysterious," said Wesley.

Hurricane nodded.

"I guess it is, in a funny sort of a way."

"Got a name?" asked Wesley.

"No."

"An address?"

"No."

"Could be tricky. Anyway, go on, tell me all about it."

"Well, it's like this," said Hurricane. "I keep seeing this girl and when she's there I..."

The next day Ambrose and Walsh were towering over FT's doorway when he answered an early knocking at the front of the house. FT was pleased. These two big ex-fast bowlers were men to listen to. They were great bowlers – not good but great. To FT and all of the West Indian people, they were icons of the game of cricket. As selectors they had a roving role to look after the bowlers in particular, while Richards and Lara took care of the batsmen.

The two big men decided to wander to the beach when FT told them Hurricane was down there. They wanted to talk to him. He was being hailed as the best prospect since Archibald, joining the great tradition of West Indies fast bowlers – Learie Constantine, Roy Gilchrist, Wesley Hall, Charlie Griffith, Andy Roberts, Michael Holding, Joel Garner, Colin Croft, Malcolm Marshall, Courtney Walsh, Curtly Ambrose, Fish Archibald. The two big men just needed to check he was OK, that the pressure of public expectation was not getting to the kid. They wanted to keep him happy – make sure he was enjoying his cricket.

They did not expect Hurricane to be beset by other concerns – different but bigger worries.

Distracted with the same thoughts of how to get to the mystery girl, Hurricane sat on the hull of *The Hurricane* and stared out over the beckoning turquoise colours of the Caribbean Sea. He did not even notice as the two ex-fast bowlers meandered towards him across Treasure Beach's charcoal-coloured sand.

Wesley had been no help, he thought. The policeman had ended up teasing him about being smitten with the girl. That's exactly why he had not gone into it with FT. They did not understand, though. It was more than that, more than just liking her. He needed her – needed her to feel good and bowl well and to feel right in a way he could not understand.

A couple of cumulus clouds flitted across the horizon. Apart from that everything was blue. It was a beautiful day.

Hurricane turned as he heard the now familiar voices. The two men were approaching the boat. Though their sporting careers were behind them now, the men looked lithe and fit. Hurricane recognized them and smiled. He stood to greet them and they all shook hands. All in their bare feet on the sands, Hurricane was easily the tallest. Hurricane even looked down on Curtly Ambrose. Not many people did.

"We just came to see how you were," said Walsh.

"How you're feeling," said Ambrose.

"I'm OK," said Hurricane.

Walsh played with the sand with his foot.

"FT says something is troubling you," he said, looking at the boy.

Hurricane looked out across the water.

The two men looked at him, waiting.

"Tell us what's up," said Ambrose. "That's what we're here for."

Hurricane sighed and sat back down on the boat. He looked up at his heroes.

"Have either of you ever needed something – you know, something outside yourselves – to make you bowl fast?" Hurricane began.

The two men nodded, listening sympathetically. They knew exactly what he was talking about – the mysterious force one called upon as a fast bowler when the moment came to dig deeper for extra strength.

"Go on," said Courtney.

He told them his problem. He told them all about the mystery girl. He told them the whole story, about the times he had seen her, about the times he had bowled badly because she seemed to be absent.

"I hope she turns up for the last two Test matches," he concluded forlornly. "It's weird. It's as if she is the force which allows me to bowl fast."

The two men looked at each other knowingly, but with sympathy.

"It's no wonder you want to find this girl," said Courtney.

"What do you mean?" said Hurricane.

"It sounds like you've fallen in love," said Curtly.

12

Record Breakers

Fourth Test at The Kensington Oval, Bridgetown, Barbados

First Day

Lara looked across the ground. Those menacing clouds were coming nearer and nearer. Charlie Constantine stood beside him and his eyes followed Lara's to the black sky which was advancing towards The Kensington Oval. The last thing he wanted in his first Test as captain was a rain delay. He knew when it rained in Barbados, it rained cats and dogs.

"The weather might make this game even harder to win," he said. "The weathermen did say it could be shortened by rain. Let's hope Fish and Hurricane are at their best."

Lara nodded.

"If we win this one we're back to all square. I wouldn't have bet on that after the first two Tests."

Charlie Constantine left him and went out to the middle and tossed up with Fitzwilliam Darcy. Darcy won the toss and elected to bowl first.

"Mind you," he said, looking at the blackness

sweeping towards them, "I'm not sure how much cricket we're going to get in today."

Where was she? Where was the mystery girl? That was all Hurricane could think as he scanned this huge and heaving, noisy and excited crowd from the West Indies dressing-room balcony.

"Worrying about that girl again," said Walsh with concern, but he was more bothered about the weather sweeping in from the west. It looked like rain to him. He hoped this would not scupper their chances to square the series. So many people had turned up, too, and the Caribbean was gripped by this series in a way it had not been for some time. Two-one down and two to play.

Hurricane felt a splash of water on his arm.

"That's the first drop," he said to Courtney Walsh.

"I've got a feeling we could be in for a long wait," said the big man.

The inevitable torrents followed soon afterwards. The groundstaff rushed around trying to cover the playing area as best they could while the players sat in the dressing-room all day and stared at the rain coming down. The disappointed crowd huddled in the stands and kept their spirits up by playing music, but eventually they started to disperse as it became clear there would be no play today.

The England selectors and players were quite

happy. They had had enough of Hurricane Hamish and Fish Archibald after the third Test – and they led the series, so the rain was quite a relief. A draw would do nicely for them in this game. Eventually the umpires called off play for the day and all the players left the ground for the hotel. With so much expectation surrounding the match, this rain was a huge disappointment to the public.

Second Day

It rained and it rained and it rained. The outfield looked like a lake. The players went to the ground, but they left very soon afterwards as, by lunch-time, the umpires had already given up on any chance of play for the day. Birds bathed in the pools on the covers on the square and two dogs splashed around on the outfield.

Hurricane could not settle to anything. He wandered between rooms in the team hotel, looking in on people for a chat, sitting watching TV with anyone and everyone, mooching around the lobby to peer outside into the street on the off chance he might see the mystery girl.

All the West Indies players were tense and fed up because of the rain. Even if it cleared up for tomorrow, they would have to beat England in three days to level the series – a tall order by any measure.

In desperation Hurricane called up *The Caribbean*

Chronicle in Jamaica. He was put straight through to the editor, Harry Hack.

"Hurricane. How lovely to speak to you. Last time I saw you we were both in court. Sorry about all this dreadful rain. What can I do for you?"

In his tense state, Hurricane started to talk too quickly. He was making no sense at all.

"I need a favour, Harry. For you to print something in the paper asking a mystery girl to come to the game and then to make sure she's definitely going to be there and then it'll be OK with my bowling and then..."

Hurricane was babbling. The editor chuckled.

"That reminds me," he said, interrupting Hurricane's garbled words. "The secret correspondent guessed you might call."

"What? He must be a mind-reader," said Hurricane, astonished.

"Yes. Anyway. I was told to give you a message that your friend will be there for the last two days of the game."

Hurricane could not believe his ears. This was weird. All he could say was: "Thank you. We may just have a chance then."

"Good luck," shouted Harry Hack, before Hurricane hung up.

Hurricane put the phone down and noticed that Fish Archibald was standing at his elbow.

"You look like you just saw a ghost," said Fish.

"I did. Sort of. Good news, though."

"Better news than this weather, you mean," said Fish.

Hurricane looked glum again. He looked out of the window at the huge puddles in the street.

"It's still raining."

"It's easing off," said Fish.

"I can't stand this," Hurricane said helplessly. "What if it doesn't clear up?"

"It will," said Fish.

"How do you know?" said Hurricane.

"I just have a feeling about this game – a good feeling. A good feeling about you and me. We're going to make those English boys hop around a little."

Hurricane grinned. Fish had a very intense look in his eyes.

Rough Tungsten was relaxing in a bath at the hotel when Rich Vermin called from Jamaica. This weather had really been a bonus. Surely there was no way the West Indies would win from here.

"Is it still raining?" growled Rich.

"Still hosing down, boss," said Rough. "No sign of it stopping either. The ground is waterlogged, anyway."

"Do we need to put another plan into action?" said Rich.

Rough could hear him munching on some food.

"No. Let's not take the risk of getting caught. Look. The game's not even started and we've lost two days. How on earth are the West Indies going to win from here? This one has a draw written all over it."

Rich Vermin belched down the line.

"You better be right, Tungsten – or you're in deep trouble."

The phone slammed down. Rough replaced his receiver gently and pushed his rubber duck through the bubbles, but his nerves were starting to jangle again.

Third Day

It dawned sunny and bright with not a wisp of cloud and the players and the spectators hurried to the ground to see if it was fit to play. The outfield was still very wet, though, and would take some time to dry out. The umpires went out for regular inspections. Around half the time was lost but the powerful Barbados sun dried the ground and it was ready for play by the middle of the day. So two and a half days – half of the Test match – had been lost to the weather and the West Indies had only this limited amount of time to try to square the series.

There were some team changes. Knightley was out for England with a bad back – Bill Eliot got his first Test chance of the tour. Churchill had a virus, so second-choice keeper Harry Crawford got his opportunity, and Collins had shin-splints, which meant a recall for Ferrers. The West Indies had preferred the seamer Padmore to spinner Frankie Genus and Radwick Scorpio replaced the disgraced Otis Campbell and was making his début as a West Indies opening batsman.

Although it had been over two days ago, the result of the toss stood, and West Indies were to take first knock. Hurricane was pleased. He wanted the ground to dry out before he had to bowl in his bare feet.

There was only one way the West Indies would have a chance of winning this game – and that was to post a big score very quickly. Charlie told Radwick Scorpio to go for all his shots.

"We've got only half the time in the match to play with, Radwick, so we need quick runs. Let's see if we can get some momentum going which our middle order can build on."

Scorpio had been in fine form for Trinidad and he loved nothing more than instructions to attack the bowling. He was not interested in the fine reputation of Willoughby and he went after his and Wickham's bowling with a relish which set the tone for the day. Charlie started quickly, too, but played one from Wickham on to his stumps on 24. Then the big Barbadian Roger Matthews came in and was soon hitting the England bowlers to all corners of The Kensington Oval, his home ground. West Indies lost Scorpio for a dynamic 68, but James came in to bat at his usual spot at number 4 and continued the attack with his island team-mate. West Indies had the flying start which they needed – by the close of play they were already 180 for 2.

Charlie Constantine sat with Fish Archibald and Hurricane Hamish long after everyone else had changed into their West Indies team uniform and had left the dressing-room. He was delighted with the way his batsmen had performed – making assured but quick runs. He knew, however, that only his bowlers could win him this match.

"Our only chance to win this game," he said, "is with some very risky declarations. I'm going to do it though – and by so doing risk a lot of criticism. The reason I'm doing it is because of you two. If you respond with good bowling, we can still win this match."

Hurricane felt sick in the pit of his stomach. Cricket was such a nerve-racking game like that – in your own performance you also made or broke the reputation of the team, and of your captain. Moreover, he had not seen the mystery girl all day. Still, the secret correspondent had said not to expect her until the last two days.

Fish Archibald just looked very calm and very determined.

"Don't worry, Charlie," he said. "You can depend on us."

Hurricane nodded, but he swallowed nervously and his guts were churning.

Fourth Day

The ground was back to its dry best for the fourth day. The batting fireworks continued in the morning and after lunch as the West Indies pushed the scoring rate along, each of the main batsmen playing useful innings and shots all round the wicket. Matthews made a cracking century, much to the delight of the Barbados crowd, and Brian Goldman looked in lovely form for a very elegant 67. Throughout the innings the West Indies scored at more than four runs an over – dynamic stuff for a Test match. Charlie eventually declared and called them in with the score at 333 for 6.

Just before the West Indies were about to take the field, there was a knock at the door. Charlie opened it. Harry Hack stood there. He had flown in for the final two days. Charlie frowned – it was no time for an interruption.

"Sorry, Charlie," said Harry, handing him a small envelope. "But just pass this on to the boy Hurricane, will you. Message from the secret correspondent."

Charlie took the envelope, eyeing it suspiciously. He went over to Hurricane.

"For you," he said. "Come on then lads, time we were out there. Enjoy your cricket."

Hurricane smiled sheepishly and stuffed the envelope in his pocket.

Charlie Constantine proudly led the team out in his first match as captain. As the crowd roared their heroes on to the ground Hurricane hung back at the end of the line and scanned the crowd. He could not see the mystery girl anywhere.

Fish's first over was fantastic – Smith and Martin only scurrying one leg-bye, so Hurricane would be bowling at Smithy.

As he made his way up from long leg, he quickly opened the envelope and read the message inside.

Look up into the Sir Garfield Sobers pavilion. You will see her there.

Hurricane looked over to the pavilion, named after the greatest player in the history of the game. There she was, just as promised, sitting in a seat right on the top tier, waving both arms above her head to him. He smiled and felt the confidence seep through him.

So the battle was resumed again. Hurricane, the young West Indian fast bowler, to bowl to Smithy Smith, the hard-hitting England opener. Both had already made an extraordinary impact in this series. The crowd was hushed.

Hurricane ran in, his bare feet eating up the ground, and ripped his fingers across the seam as he bowled the ball with all his might. It was just on a length, hit the seam and moved from leg to off. Smith tried to drive it down the ground, but the movement deceived him. The ball took a thick outside edge and flew like a tracer bullet wide to the right of Joel James at third slip, who dived and took a magnificent, one-handed tumbling catch. England were 1 for 1 and Smith, their most dangerous player, was on his way back to the pavilion.

Hurricane Hamish and Fish Archibald were devastating that afternoon. Charlie rotated them with Amory, Padmore and King, but Hurricane and Fish did the bulk of the bowling. After Smith was out, the procession began, as the Englishmen failed to deal with the pace of the West Indies express fast bowlers on this lively Barbados track.

Hurricane bowled as fast and as straight as he could ever remember bowling. Today, he just seemed able to put the ball exactly where he wanted to. Fish was also bowling beautifully, with a lot of sideways movement, varying his pace and keeping the English batsmen guessing. He was still a very fit man and he and Hurricane ran in gamely and tirelessly in the stultifying heat, with only one thing on their minds – they had to get amongst the English batting to have any chance of a win in this shortened game.

By the end of the day England had slumped to 185 for 8 – only the solid Martin and gritty Darcy offering any resistance. Fish and Hurricane already had four wickets each.

Despite such a successful day, time was short for the West Indies. There was only a day left and Charlie Constantine would have his work cut out to conjure a win from here.

Fifth Day

England managed to hang around for another half an hour, but Fish bowled Wentworth and Hurricane got Willoughby caught behind. The two fast bowlers each finished with a five-wicket haul. England were all out for 200 – 133 behind on the first innings.

Now was the moment of truth for Charlie. He needed as much time as possible to bowl England out. However, if he made an early declaration there was also the danger of allowing England in for the win which would clinch the series.

He and Scorpio went in and blazed away for a quick 50 in only thirty minutes. At this point, Charlie shocked everyone by declaring the West Indies innings closed. England would need only 184 to win, in about two sessions and 45 minutes – or around seventy overs – easily enough time to get the runs.

"I know the risk," he told his team. "Equally we need some time to bowl them out – and I want to level this series and go to the last Test all square. We'll go for broke. Win or lose."

He looked to his bowlers, especially Fish and Hurricane.

"It's up to you now. I want you to throw everything you've got at them."

Charlie felt that again the key confrontation might be Hurricane versus Smithy Smith. He knew that if Smith got going then England would probably knock these runs off without too much trouble. They needed him out early.

Hurricane was pleased to see the mystery girl still in her position in the pavilion. His first ball to Smith was short and quick. Smith rocked back on to his toes and played a majestic square cut wide of point for four. This was ominous, thought Charlie Constantine. He noticed that Hurricane looked very relaxed though and did not seem in the least bit bothered.

Smith expected a bouncer in retaliation, but, in turn, Hurricane knew he would be anticipating this. He pitched the next one right up in the block-hole and it hit Smith full on the toe. As one the West Indies team went up in a massive shout for lbw. Hurricane turned and bellowed at Umpire Murray.

"Howzaaaaaaaaaaaaaaaattttttttttttttttttt!!!"

Murray looked long and hard for what seemed like an age, then, like a gunfighter drawing a pistol, he raised his right index finger to send Smith on his way. England 6 for 1. Smith out for only 4. Suddenly the West Indies team and the noisy Barbados crowd began to scent victory.

Charlie Constantine worked Fish and Hurricane hard. Wickets fell regularly, and Roy Amory bowled very tightly in support, but England also kept up with the rate, picking up runs from any loose deliveries. Bingley made a dogged 32 before Fish got one to flick his glove on the way through to Andy Alleyne. At the other end Darcy had been playing his shots to progress to his second fifty of the match. He looked as though he might see England home, until he flicked at one down the leg side, and Alleyne took a brilliant catch flying to his left.

Bertram managed only 4 and when Wentworth went for 3 England were 158 for 8. Two wickets left. 26 runs needed, but with Harry Crawford looking fairly comfortable on 18 not out.

Crawford boldly hooked Fish's next ball down past long leg for 4. 22 needed. Constantine placed a second man down on the fence behind square on the leg side. Fish dug in another short one. Crawford was on to it too late and he skied it high in the air towards fine leg, where Sherwin Padmore took an excellent running catch. West Indies needed only one more wicket to win.

Willoughby, not noted for his batting ability, came in to join Wickham. They scrambled a leg-bye off the last ball of Fish Archibald's over and Willoughby kept the strike. 21 needed for England. One wicket for West Indies. Hurricane Hamish to bowl to John Willoughby.

Hurricane flew across the ground and hurled down a full-pitched ball on off stump. Willoughby prodded at it and edged it out past the slips for 4. 17 needed.

Hurricane returned to his mark. Things were getting too tense. He knew he had to finish it now.

"Pitch it up," said Fish, handing Hurricane the ball. "Full length – fast and straight."

Hurricane raced in. He really bent his back for this one, nearly stumbling to the ground in his effort. Willoughby never saw it. As Hurricane looked up in his follow-through all he could see was timber flying everywhere. The next thing he knew he was surrounded by his overjoyed team-mates. West Indies had won the most improbable of victories.

Hurricane had hardly noticed during the drama of the match that he and Fish had taken all the wickets. Five wickets in both innings and ten wickets in the match to each of them represented a success and a symmetry never seen before on the Test match stage. Fish got the Man of the Match award, but, as he said to Hurricane: "This belongs to both of us. I only wish I'd been able to bowl like you at your age."

What made Hurricane happiest of all was that Charlie was being acclaimed for his courage in the two declarations he made in the match. He had been prepared to put his neck on the block and Hurricane had not let him down. That made Hurricane feel good. After all, without Charlie, and without the faith he had shown in him – by giving him his own trial in the first place and then picking him for Jamaica – Hurricane knew that he would not even be here.

The series was level at two-two, with one match to play.

The Conch Bar, Kingston, Jamaica

Rough had never seen Rich Vermin so angry as he called him every name under the sun and ranted and raved like a crazy man. Rich could sense his one million pounds slipping away and he blamed Rough. It was bad enough that the English couple he had hired had been found out; it was even worse that Otis had run away, depriving them of their insider; but, for Rough to promise him, quite wrongly, that the rain would ensure a draw – now that was the last straw.

"You idiot. You buffoon. You..."

"I'm sorry, Rich. I've said I'm sorry. I'd spoken to the weather centre and everything. It looked like a total wash-out."

Rich Vermin's face was getting redder and redder and looked set to explode.

"Well," he said, looking round the bar to see if anyone was listening. "Sorry means nothing."

Rough stared glumly into his beer.

"How was I supposed to know Archibald and Hamish would bowl like men possessed? I've been watching cricket a long time and I've never seen anything like it."

Rich snarled.

"This has all started going wrong since that lanky kid got in the team. We were fine for the first two Tests."

Rough nodded.

"I know," he said.

It was true – Hurricane was making the difference.

"Well," said Rough, between clenched teeth. "I'm not having some child losing me my million."

"How can we stop him?" said Rough. "It's hopeless."

Rich Vermin glared at Rough.

"I've told you – nothing gets in my way!"

Rough looked sick.

"Have you got another plan?" he asked tentatively.

"You bet I have," said Rich Vermin. "The perfect plan."

He started to laugh for the first time in days.

FOURTH TEST SCORECARD

West Indies

	1st Innings				2nd Innings		
C Constantine*		b Wickham	24		not out		20
R Z Scorpio	c Crawford	b Wentworth	68		not out		29
R P Matthews	c Crawford	b Bertram	113				
J J James		b Darcy	22				
B Goldman	c Eliot	b Willoughby	67				
A C Alleyne+		not out	15				
L V A King	lbw	b Wickham	8				
S T Padmore		not out	4				
R P B Amory							
F S Archibald							
H Hamish							
Extras	(b3, lb5, nb3, w1)		12	(lb1)			1

Total (for 6 declared) **333**   (all out) **50**

Fall of Wickets   1-59,2-135,3-190,4-223,5-287,6-319

Bowling	O	M	R	W	O	M	R	W
J Willoughby	15	3	67	1	3	0	13	0
G D Wickham	23	5	61	2	2	0	15	0
E L Bertram	14	0	72	1	2	0	16	0
F R Wentworth	13	0	92	1				
F W Darcy	15	3	33	1	1	0	5	0

England

	1st Innings				2nd Innings		
S T L Smith	c James	b Hamish	0	lbw		b Hamish	4
R Martin	c Alleyne	b Archibald	61	c Scorpio		b Hamish	11
E S Ferrers	c Matthews	b Archibald	13			b Archibald	1
C P Bingley	c Alleyne	b Hamish	24	c Alleyne		b Archibald	32
W A Eliot	lbw	b Hamish	8	lbw		b Archibald	17
F W Darcy*		b Archibald	59	c Alleyne		b Archibald	63
E L Bertram	c Archibald	b Hamish	3	lbw		b Hamish	4
F R Wentworth		b Archibald	18	c Alleyne		b Hamish	3
H P Crawford+	lbw	b Archibald	0	c Padmore		b Archibald	22
G D Wickham		not out	0			not out	0
J Willoughby	c Alleyne	b Hamish	7			b Hamish	4
Extras	(b1, lb2, nb4)		7	(b1, lb4, nb1)			6

Total (all out) **200**   (all out) **167**

Fall of Wickets   1-1,2-37,3-90,4-104,5-134,
6-146,7-175,8-185,9-189,10-200   1-6,2-26,3-32,4-79,5-112,
6-133,7-138,8-158,9-162,10-167

Bowling	O	M	R	W	O	M	R	W
F S Archibald	15	3	39	5	18	1	57	5
H Hamish	18.4	2	78	5	15.2	4	46	5
R P B Amory	9	3	32	0	13	2	26	0
S T Padmore	12	0	32	0	3	1	10	0
L V A King	9	0	16	0	12	0	21	0
R Z Scorpio					2	1	2	0

Man of the Match: F S Archibald (West Indies)
West Indies won by 16 runs

13

The Blue Mountains

Treasure Beach, Jamaica

The excitement had completely enveloped the island of Jamaica, and for Hurricane it was like a dream come true. Tomorrow was the deciding Test in the series versus England – to be on his home ground at Kingston. In fact, almost every man, woman and child in the whole of the West Indies could only talk about one thing – the cricket. Could their team beat England at Sabina Park and win the series three matches to two, having been trailing two-nil? If they did so they would make history.

Everyone wanted to talk to Hurricane and the only escape from the clamour was back with everyday life at Treasure Beach with FT.

Today was a normal morning – or as normal as it could be with the deciding Test almost upon them – and Hurricane was walking down the black sand to the boat, planning to get right away from everything with some solitary fishing on the Pedro Banks. It was dawn – Hurricane had been waking early with the excitement about the coming match – and he planned a quick hour or two's fishing to bring FT back something tasty for him to cook for their breakfast. The beach was deserted, just the noise of the sea and some gulls doing their own fishing, swooping above the waves. The sun was hardly up, but it was already hot. Today would be a scorcher – just how Hurricane liked it.

Hurricane wandered towards the boat. He chuckled to himself – it was a good job Judge Herring could not see him now. He imagined the great booming voice telling him off: "A boy of twelve – alone – fishing the Pedro Banks." Still, the old judge had been OK in the end and had let him play for his country.

As he neared the boat he sensed something unusual, felt a strange uneasiness. He thought suddenly that he was not alone. He could not see anyone, but he felt the presence of someone. He looked back along the beach the way he had come and all he could see were his own footprints. Before him were just the rocks and the boat *The Hurricane* tucked in its usual place before them. Probably just nerves about the Test match, he thought.

He was just nearing the boat, still feeling slightly apprehensive, when the two men lunged at him. They had been lying in the sand, hidden between the rocks and the hull of *The Hurricane*. He hardly saw them before they were upon him and before he could resist he took a blow to the head which seemed to make his skull explode. Suddenly everything was blackness.

The short plank which Rich Vermin hit him with had knocked the boy unconscious immediately. Hurricane teetered and fell to the ground. Vermin grinned and spat on to the sand.

"That'll teach him to take ten wickets in a match," he roared.

Rough Tungsten laughed nervously.

"Nice work, Rich," he said.

"Let's see if we can move the lanky fool," said Rich Vermin.

The two men tried to lift the boy into the boat. He was so long and tall it was all they could do to move him, but they hefted and struggled and finally managed to tip him into it. Then they dragged the boat to the water, groaning and grunting with the effort. Rich Vermin was wet with sweat and his huge belly wobbled like jelly with the effort. Rough Tungsten's eyes were nearly popping out of his head with the strain. They managed to get the boat down to the water and both climbed in clumsily. Rough Tungsten sat at the stern and started up the engine. Hurricane did not stir.

"I hope you didn't hit him too hard, Rich," Rough said nervously. "He's out cold."

"What if I did? He's caused us enough trouble," growled the fat man, slumped in the bow mopping the sweat from round his face. "Just shut up and get us there, will you?"

Rich Vermin stared at Hurricane, slumped life-lessly in the bottom of the boat.

"Not such a great fast bowler lying there like that are you?" he said to the unconscious body.

FT woke and ambled out into the kitchen to make himself a pot of Blue Mountain coffee. There was a note on the table from Hurricane.

Gone to catch our breakfast. Get ready to cook me something special. I need my strength for tomorrow.

FT smiled. The cheek of the boy.

He made his coffee and sat down to wait. Hurricane was getting up so early these days he would be back with the morning catch anytime now.

The time passed, though, and FT started to wonder where the boy had got to. Oh well, Hurricane was always late...

More time passed and he started to get a little worried. He went to the front door and looked along the dirt track down to the beach, but there was no sign of Hurricane making his way home. There was only one thing for it, he'd have to take a walk out to the beach himself. It was probably nothing – he was just taking longer than usual to catch something worth eating – but nevertheless FT felt a bit concerned, uneasy inside. Maybe I'm just nervous about the Test tomorrow, he thought. He was so keen for Hurricane to do well.

There was no sign of the boat down at the beach. Hurricane was obviously still out fishing. The sun was rising higher out to the east.

More time passed. FT was very fidgety by now.

What on earth was Hurricane playing at – today of all days? If there was no catch to be had he should have left it. They didn't need to have fish after all. FT strained his eyes from his vantage point out to sea. There was nothing, no sign of the boat at all. Where are you Hurricane, for goodness' sake?

FT looked down the beach and was shocked to see the unmistakable figure of Wesley Clarke hurrying towards him. As the policeman got nearer FT could see the look of concern on his face. Increasingly, FT felt that horrible sense that something was badly wrong.

"I thought I'd find you here," said Wesley breathlessly, as he approached. "I went to your house but you weren't there."

"What's up, Wesley?"

"No sign of Hurricane?"

"No. What's going on?" FT asked.

Wesley took a deep breath. It seemed to be his role to the bearer of bad news these days.

"I just got a call at the station. Someone found

Hurricane's boat, abandoned miles down the coast at Black River Bay."

FT shuddered.

"No sign of Hurricane?"

"None," said Wesley desperately.

The two men were silent, their minds racing, their hearts pounding.

"It can't be an accident," said FT. "He just handles a boat too well. It's calm out on the water today, too."

Wesley nodded, running his fingers nervously through his hair. "That's what I thought. And he'd have no cause to go down to Black River. Anyway, Hurricane wouldn't just take off like that without letting you know. Not the day before the big game."

FT had gone white as a sheet.

"What if somebody is trying to harm him?" he murmured.

"But it doesn't make sense," said Wesley. "He's the hero of the island."

Fear filled FT's soul.

"Maybe someone's trying to stop him playing again," he said.

The men were silent.

"There's only one thing for it," said Wesley. "I'll have to ring *The Caribbean Chronicle* and get Harry Hack to call on the people to search for him. Come on, let's go."

"Good thinking," said FT, but there was strain all

over his face and his eyes were dark with concern. The two men set out back along the beach to the village.

Black River Bay, Jamaica

Rich Vermin and Rough Tungsten had taken the boat the few miles west round the coast to Black River Bay. It would fool people – it was the wrong direction from Treasure Beach for where they were finally heading. By the time they got to Black River Hurricane was starting to move and moan, but, before he came round, they got him out of the boat and into the back of the black van which was waiting there. Rough Tungsten tied his ankles and his wrists with rope and locked the door. He and Rich climbed into the front of the van and Rough gunned the engine and drove off at great speed.

The movement of the van gradually shook Hurricane awake. As he began to regain consciousness, all he could sense was the darkness, that he was tied up and that he was in a moving vehicle. He remembered being leapt on by two men and struck with something. The world was still spinning and a huge lump was growing on his forehead.

I've been kidnapped, he thought.

He groaned and moaned as he was bounced around in the back of the van. He felt sick from the blow on the head and the ropes were rubbing wounds on his skin. Though he was groggy he could think of only one thing – how was he going to make it to the ground tomorrow if these villains were intent on keeping him captive?

The Blue Mountains, Jamaica

Eventually, after what seemed like an age, the van stopped. Hurricane heard noises as the men got out and he heard the bolts on the door slide back. Suddenly he was blinded by light as the back door of the van was swung open. As he blinked to adjust to the light and slowly opened his eyes, he saw an ugly fat man, pointing a gun at him. Beside him stood another man, a small figure, who seemed to be twitching with nerves.

"Get out, baby-face," said Rich, violently.

Rough reached in and grabbed the rope which was round Hurricane's wrists. Hurricane slid across the van and Rough yanked him out and Hurricane fell heavily on to the stony ground. The two men looked down at him – the fat man laughing loudly now, the small man grinning nervously.

"What do you want with me?" said Hurricane.

They ignored him.

Hurricane looked around. All he could see were thickets and trees and a beautiful view down into the valleys. They seemed to be up in the mountains. Close by there was a barn tucked away in a copse.

"Untie his legs," said Rich.

Rough untied the ropes on his legs and pulled Hurricane to his feet. Rich Vermin was still pointing the gun at him. Rough took his arm and led him away from the van. He took him towards the barn.

Inside the barn it was empty – just straw on the floor and empty iron animal troughs around the perimeter. Rich indicated with the gun for Hurricane to sit upon a bale of hay.

"Where are we?" asked Hurricane angrily.

He was starting to feel a little less groggy.

"A long way from Sabina Park, you idiot boy," said Rich. "Nobody will find you up here before tomorrow. No Test match for you."

They had driven him miles – all the way across the island and beyond Kingston and up into the Blue Mountains. Hurricane was still trying to take it all in.

"Why are you keeping me here?"

Rich Vermin just laughed.

"Oh, you poor stupid boy," he said. "Haven't you worked out that someone is not too keen on you playing for the West Indies?"

The snarl in the tone of the man made something occur to Hurricane, triggered something in his memory.

"Hold on," he said. "I recognize your voice."

Hurricane was remembering the court hearing.

Rich laughed again. It was the laugh that really gave him away.

"That laugh," said Hurricane. "It was on the tape in the court."

Hurricane knew now who he was – the villain talking to the couple on the tape Harry Hack had played.

"You must have been the one plotting with that English couple to pretend I was theirs."

Rich snarled: "You're cleverer than you look."

"Yes," said Hurricane. "I know who you are. You're the one who paid that couple to come to the court and try to con everyone."

"Very good, little boy. You've got the picture."

Rich was still pointing the gun at him.

"And you," said Hurricane angrily to Rough Tungsten. "I know your face from the group of press men. You're that one who always writes that rubbish in *The West Indies Wayfarer*, aren't you. Blimey – I wish FT was here. He can't stand you."

Rough chuckled in his excitement.

"Oh, we've got lots of stories to tell you about what we've been up to," he said. "Shall I tell him, Rich?"

Rich laughed: "Why not? We'll be long gone before anyone finds him."

"What things?" demanded Hurricane.

"Oh, little things that have been going on in this series," said Rich. "Little difficulties the poor sad West Indies team have encountered."

"What?" cried Hurricane.

Rough giggled again, but could not resist taunting Hurricane with tales of their conspiracies.

"Otis put the devil's potion in people's drinks; I shone magic mirrors into batsmen's eyes; I stole Clarke's secret file on you and that old MCC towel; Rich, here, bribed that nice little English couple to say they were your parents; Otis tried to make you lot lose with his tactics; Rich and I..."

As Rough rambled on, chattering like an agitated monkey, Hurricane was taking it all in.

So Charlie had been right about him and some of the other batsmen being drugged in the first Test. Then they had light flashed into their eyes in the second Test! Hence the low scores. And Otis actually had been trying to make his own team struggle. It explained a few things. There had been people trying all along to keep Hurricane out of the side and there had been a plot to try to make the West Indies lose.

He stared at the two men in disgust.

"You've tried most things," said Hurricane. "You won't stop us, though. We're still going to win."

"Well, my little boy," laughed Rich Vermin, pointing his gun at him again. "That's why you're here. One thing is for sure. You won't be playing in this match. Smithy should like that. And England should like it. And England will win. And I will have one million pounds."

Hurricane looked on in anger as the fat man started to shake with laughter.

Harry Hack put out a special edition of the newspaper that afternoon, with the front page headline: *SUSPECTED KIDNAP – HURRICANE HAMISH IS MISSING!* He called on the Jamaican people to keep their eyes peeled and to report any mysterious sightings or anyone behaving suspiciously straight to the police. In response many people took to the streets, scoured the beaches and asked around the town to help the police in their search.

The barn was hidden away, though, in a very secluded and inaccessible part of the Blue Mountains. It would take a long time for anyone to find Hurricane.

Darkness was coming and things seemed increasingly hopeless.

As night started to fall, Hurricane sat alone, tied up in the barn, unable to move. The two men had left him, saying they would return in the morning. He had tried shouting out but his voice just echoed around the locked barn. He could not do anything to loosen or try and cut the ropes, which now tied him to an animal feeding rack. They had left him sitting on the floor in the straw, like an animal himself. His limbs ached like crazy from the position he was in.

He felt despair sit more and more heavily upon

his shoulders. Outside, the wind whistled through the mountains and wild animals called out in the blackness. He felt in pain and alone and a little scared. He knew FT would be sick with worry. He knew he would be letting the whole team down.

He dropped his head on to his chest in anguish and willed someone – anyone – to find a way to get to him.

14

The Black Van

The Conch Bar, Kingston, Jamaica

The whole of Jamaica might have been looking for him, but no one was going to find Hurricane where he was. Everyone had a short night and got up at the crack of dawn to scour the island. Meanwhile the clock was ticking and the start of the Test match loomed ever closer.

It seemed hopeless, and the whisper went around the community that Hurricane had not been found and was bound to miss the game. One person, though, had a hunch – just maybe there was a way to trace him.

The black van parked outside The Conch Bar confirmed the mystery girl's suspicions. It would be highly likely that Rich Vermin would be in there at this time of day. On entering the place, now serving huge morning breakfasts, it was no surprise to see Rich Vermin and Rough Tungsten at their usual table in the corner.

She had been right – nothing would keep Rich Vermin from his breakfast. There he was tucking into his usual morning helping of four fried eggs, eight rashers of bacon, six large pork sausages and half a loaf of toast – all washed down with some very sugary tea.

The two men were speaking in whispers. The mystery girl took a table across the room from them, ordered a coffee and waited to see what their next move might be. Perhaps they might lead the trail to Hurricane Hamish.

While Rich and Rough were finishing their breakfast, the mystery girl's mind was working fast. Their body language, their furtive whispering, their excitement and their nervous glancing around the room seemed to indicate that they indeed might be up to something. There was only one thing for it – to call Harry Hack.

The mystery girl quickly got some change from the barman and dialled *The Caribbean Chronicle* from the phone in the corner. As usual, she slipped very easily into the disguised voice of the secret correspondent.

Harry Hack was surprised to get the phone call. "Oh, it's you. Thought you would be at the ground by now."

"I need you to do something for me, urgently. I think I can get to Hurricane Hamish."

"Good grief," said Harry. "Are you sure?"

"As much as I can be. I need to have a note delivered to Charlie Constantine to ensure he keeps Hurricane's place in the team open for him."

There was a pause from Harry Hack at the other end of the line.

"But it's not long before the game starts."

"I know, but it'll be worth it if Hurricane can get there. I'm going to leave a note for Charlie with the barman. Would you come and pick it up and deliver it to him at the ground as fast as you possibly can?"

"Sure. I can do all that from here in ten or fifteen minutes."

"Perfect. Thanks, Harry. I appreciate it."

Harry sighed.

"Well we all want to win this match – and if there's a chance of finding Hurricane and getting him to the game, I've got to go with your feelings on this."

"I won't let you down," said the familiar voice.

She scribbled a note on a piece of paper, then went to pay for the coffee and to give the note to the barman for safe keeping.

At this point Rough and Rich were just getting up to leave. Rough rubbed his belly and threw a few Jamaican dollars across the bar at the barman. He stared suspiciously at the girl standing by the bar and sneered. Hadn't he seen her in this place one time before?

"Off to the match?" asked the barman.

"He is," said Rich, pointing his thumb at Rough Tungsten. "After all, he's got to write those stupid articles of his."

Rough smiled pathetically.

"As for me," said Rich. "I've got a bit of other business to take care of. I'm going to go and watch the game on TV with a friend of mine."

At this he rocked on his heels and his flab shook as he roared with laughter. Rough Tungsten giggled nervously.

The two men left and the girl slipped out into the street behind them. They shook hands and Rough turned on his heels and headed on foot towards Sabina Park. Rich jumped into the driving seat of the black van.

At this point, she sidled up to the back of the van and tried the rear doors.

Please let them be open.

The handle moved and the door opened and quick as a flash, unnoticed by Rough Tungsten as he disappeared down the street and unheard by Rich Vermin as he started the engine, the mystery girl jumped into the van and shut the door in an instant. Now surely Rich Vermin might lead the way to Hurricane Hamish.

The journey took some time. The mystery girl was bounced around in the dark in the back of the van. The engine groaned and roared as Rich Vermin constantly changed gear – they seemed to be on a winding road and also to be climbing up into the hills.

The Blue Mountains, thought the mystery girl –

that's where they've taken him and kept him. They've kidnapped him to stop him playing and are keeping him somewhere up in the Blue Mountains.

The Blue Mountains, Jamaica

After what seemed like an age, the van jerked to a halt. The engine stopped and all of a sudden there was a deathly quiet. The mystery girl heard Rich Vermin get out of the van, slam the driver's door and heard his footsteps shuffling along on some stony ground.

Hoping not to be seen she opened the rear doors and jumped out, hiding dazzled eyes against the blinding sunshine after the pitch black of the van, and crouched down while adjusting to the light. It was very peaceful up here – just the noise of insects and birds. The silence was broken by a roar of laughter from not far away – that familiar, vulgar, belly-wobbling laugh of Rich Vermin.

The girl crawled to the front of the van and peered towards where Rich Vermin had walked. There was a barn with its door ajar, some lights on in there and the sound of two voices from inside – shouts and cries. One of the voices was Rich Vermin's. The other she would recognize anywhere – the voice of Hurricane Hamish shouting angrily, which, on creeping closer to the barn, could be heard more clearly.

"Let me out, you crook. You can't keep me here!"

"Oh, I can and I will!" shouted Rich Vermin. "I'll keep you for five days, because I'm going to wire up a TV and I want you to watch the game with me – as a sort of torture for you. After that I'll decide whether to let you go or not. Depending on who wins."

As Rich Vermin started to laugh again, the mystery girl could see his silhouette in the barn, his arm outstretched, a gun waving in front of him.

Sabina Park, Kingston, Jamaica

"It's a note for you, Charlie," Brian Lara said, handing Constantine the envelope. "I bumped into Harry Hack rushing to find you. He said to pass this on as a matter of urgency. Said it was from the secret correspondent. Said the result of this game depended on it."

Charlie tore open the envelope. Play was due to start very soon and there was still no sign of Hurricane Hamish. He quickly read the note:

I have gone to rescue Hurricane Hamish. Wait for him. I promise you he'll get there. He's on his way. I can assure you. Please include him in the team. You won't win without him. I'll get him to you as soon as I possibly can.

That was all the note said. Charlie Constantine frowned. He had a very important decision to make right now. Either they replaced Hurricane, and he would not be able to play if he did show up; or they could start with a substitute fielder and if Hurricane appeared he would then be able to play in the match. The risk was huge, though, because in this case the sub wouldn't be able to bat or bowl, and they would effectively be a man short for the whole match.

The other players looked up, concerned, as he finished the note. He passed it to Fish, and as it was passed round the team Charlie stood and looked out over the packed stands of Sabina Park. He had never seen the ground so overflowing with fans, never felt such an atmosphere of eager anticipation in the crowd. These people have come to see Hurricane, he thought. They believe in him and I believe in him, so I must take this chance.

"Well? What do you say, skipper?" said Fish.

The whole of the team looked at Charlie Constantine.

"I'm going to take the risk," said Charlie. "We'll name Hurricane in the side."

Fish nodded.

"You're a brave man, Charlie," he said. "But I'm sure you're doing the right thing."

"Let's just hope we can win the toss and bat," said Charlie, wistfully.

The Blue Mountains, Jamaica

It made a bizarre sight. The young West Indian boy, his feet and hands tied by rope, sitting on a bale of straw. On another bale next to him sat a huge fat villain, who had a gun resting on the straw by his side, and both of them staring at a TV, which was perched on another bale of straw. The Test match TV theme tune started up.

"Here we go," said Rich Vermin, laughing between mouthfuls of crisps. "You can watch the game you aren't playing in!"

Hurricane shifted uncomfortably on the bale.

"You won't get away with this," he said.

"Just watch me," said Rich. "You stupid boy."

The mystery girl was watching them through a crack between the planks of the barn wall. With each moment time was slipping away, but Rich Vermin's gun made a fast move impossible. This was the problem – how to get the gun, get Hurricane untied and allow him to escape.

On the outside of the barn, close to where she was crouching, was the fuse box to the barn. Maybe this would present a chance to disarm Rich Vermin. It was very dark inside the barn, as the building had no windows at all. There was a dim electric light bulb hanging on a wire down from the roof and there was the flickering light from the TV screen. She began to devise a plan.

Sabina Park, Kingston, Jamaica

Out in the middle Charlie Constantine and Fitzwilliam Darcy shook hands and exchanged team sheets before the toss. Darcy looked down the list of the West Indies eleven. He had heard the story of the missing Hurricane and was surprised to see him named in their team.

"So Hurricane Hamish is in. Is he here at the ground?"

Charlie coughed.

"He's on his way."

Darcy was thinking hard. If the boy wasn't here yet the best thing England could do would be to try to take advantage of that and get some quick runs on the board this morning. Smith could have an early thrash against their other bowlers.

Charlie tossed the Jamaican five dollar coin. As it spun in the air, Darcy called.

"Heads."

The coin landed and the two men looked down. The head of Norman W Manley, the former Jamaican statesman who had led the island to independence, stared back up at them.

"We'll have a bat," said Darcy.

The Blue Mountains, Jamaica

It was Rich Vermin's insatiable greed which made the mystery girl's move possible. As they watched the umpires walking out on to the ground on the screen, Rich stared glumly into his empty family bag of smoky bacon crisps.

"Drat," he said. "Gone and finished them. And I'm starving, too. Still, plenty more where that came from."

Food was stuck to the fat man's gold front teeth as he laughed into Hurricane's face. Hurricane turned away in disgust.

"So they've named you in the side, baby boy," spat Rich. "Smithy will enjoy the luxury of West Indies being a bowler short for the whole match."

Rich started laughing again.

"And they're batting first. A run feast. Talking of which, I need more grub," he said.

Rich picked up the gun and hauled himself to his feet.

"Don't you move," he said. "Or I'll shoot you. I'm going to get some popcorn from the van."

He lurched out of the barn and the mystery girl watched him staggering clumsily towards the black van. Now was her chance. She ripped at the wires in the fuse box and the barn was suddenly plunged into darkness. Scooting round the barn while Rich Vermin was rummaging around in the van's glove compartment, she then ran inside and shut the door. It was black as night in there.

"Hurricane?" she said.

"Who is it?" said Hurricane, bewildered by what was going on. "What's happening?"

"It's OK. Keep talking and I'll find my way over to you."

"What's going on? How did you find me? Who's there?" Hurricane called out.

Hurricane couldn't see anything, but the voice spoke to him, urging him to keep talking.

"Who is it? Who are you?" he asked, trying to peer through the murk.

By the sound of Hurricane's voice the mystery girl found him in the blackness and, untying the rope knots with great dexterity, soon had Hurricane's hands and feet free.

"Thank you," said Hurricane. He peered at the shadow in the gloom. "Who are you?" he asked again. "The mystery girl?"

"Shh. No time for that. I've got a plan to get you out of here," said the girl. "This is what we're going to do..."

Rich was pleased with what he found in the van. There was not only popcorn, but also more crisps, some chocolate and a couple of bottles of beer. This should see him through until lunch, he thought, with a sigh of satisfaction. He shut the passenger door and turned and staggered back towards the barn, sweating in the heat.

He looked up and noticed the barn door was shut. Must have blown to in the wind, he thought. He waddled up to the barn and opened the door. It was pitch black inside. He fumbled for the light switch and flicked it, but nothing happened. Rich swore.

"Oy. Hamish, you little brat. What's going on with the power. You better not be trying anything funny. I've got a gun, remember."

He started to move blindly into the barn. In the

next instant he felt a rope flung around his neck and the thud of iron on his knuckles which made the gun spin out of his hands. Then he felt the rope loosen, as the cold barrel of the gun was held against his temple.

"Don't move. Get on the floor and get your hands behind your back," said a girl's voice.

By the thin shaft of light which shone through the now-open door Hurricane started to tie Rich's hands and legs together. The mystery girl held the gun to the villain's head as Hurricane worked. Then they made Rich Vermin crawl on his elbows and knees to the animal feeding rack and, while Hurricane tied him to that, the girl ran out of the gloom to the van and, finding the keys in the ignition, started it up and backed it towards the barn.

For a moment Hurricane stood over Rich Vermin. Rich was whimpering, curled up on the ground. Hurricane grinned.

"Bye bye, Rich," he said. "Good riddance. Nice to give you a taste of your own medicine. Now you see what it's like to be treated like an animal."

Hurricane turned and ran towards the light from the door.

The van was backed up to the barn door and its rear doors were open.

"Quick," the voice shouted from the front of the van.

Without further thought, Hurricane flung himself

into the van and pulled the doors shut as it screeched away.

The black van was soon hurtling round corners down from the Blue Mountains towards Kingston. Hurricane was bounced around in the back of the van, but that didn't matter – he was going to get to the game. How many was Smith going to have notched up by now? Was it all going to be too late? At the crazy speed the van was being driven the journey wouldn't take long, anyway.

Sabina Park, Kingston, Jamaica

Hurricane opened the door and took a moment to adjust to the light. The van was parked right outside the entrance of Sabina Park. He stepped out of the van and walked to the driver's door. The door was open. Hurricane peered inside. Nothing. The mystery girl had disappeared.

Viv Richards stood at the gate to the ground, pacing back and forth and looking at his watch. He looked up and noticed the boy.

"Hey Hurricane. At last. Thank goodness you're here. Let's go."

Hurricane hesitated.

"Where did she go?" he asked, puzzled.

He looked up and down the street. It was deserted. After all, everyone was inside the ground or at home in front of the TV.

"I didn't see anyone," said Richards. "Anyway – get a move on. Smith's going berserk out there."

Hurricane was totally bemused.

"You didn't see anyone?" he asked. "Maybe a girl with long dark hair. About my age?"

Viv Richards looked at his watch again.

"Not a soul. Come on, Hurricane. Please. It's no time to be thinking about girls."

"She certainly wants to stay a mystery," said Hurricane, and he ran like crazy to the dressing-room to get changed.

15

The Left-hander

Fifth Test at Sabina Park,
Kingston, Jamaica

First Day

As it was his hundredth Test match, Fish Archibald had been given the honour of leading the West Indies out on to his home turf of Sabina Park. Charlie Constantine and the rest of the side all hung back for several moments as Fish walked out alone on to the ground. The crowd gave him a rousing reception as Jamaica paid tribute to one of her favourite sons. Fish had a tear in his eye. He could hardly believe it was his hundredth Test – it seemed like yesterday that he had been making his début over in England.

The ground had never been so busy. People were sitting on the roofs of the stand and hanging from the branches of trees that overlooked the ground. A local builder had hoisted the cage of a crane behind the pavilion and he stood in there with what must have been two dozen of his friends. It was impossible to say how many were watching, but Sabina Park was bursting at the seams. Those who were not there were crowded around TV sets at home or walking the streets with radios clasped to their ears. Nobody was at work. Everything else on the island had stopped for these five very special Test match days.

Knightley and Churchill were back for England. They were at full strength and had reverted to the side which had served them so well in the first two Test matches. West Indies were unchanged from the last Test – Hurricane Hamish named in the team, but his whereabouts still unknown.

The murmurs started as the people realized that the West Indies were taking the field with a substitute – Frankie Genus. The same conversation circulated the ground.

"Hurricane not here then?"

"No. But Constantine has named him in the team. Genus is just on to field as sub."

"Wow. That's a risk, isn't it?"

Things started badly for the West Indies. In Hurricane's absence Amory opened with Fish Archibald, but Smith, delighted at the unexpected bonus of not having to face the young fast bowler, got away to a quick start. He was supported at the other end by the rock solid defence of Robert Martin, who had been a reliable foil to Smithy the Slogger throughout the series.

Smith was playing all his shots, and Charlie Constantine needed twenty men on the field to contain him. Where are you, Hurricane? he thought to himself. Was I right to trust the secret correspondent? I hope I've not made a mistake.

Smith blazed away. The clock moved round, and the runs flowed. Smith drove past mid-off, cut behind point, glanced to fine leg, hooked to deep square leg, drove through extra cover and clipped the ball of his legs through mid-wicket. His fifty came up in only an hour. There was still no sign of Hurricane Hamish. The crowd was as quiet as a full Sabina Park had ever been.

It started as a murmur, a hum that went around the ground – then there was an eerie sort of a hush. Charlie and Fish were standing together discussing the field for the next over, but the strange silence stopped their conversation. Charlie was aware that all eyes were turned towards the pavilion and he and Fish turned in time to see the lanky figure bounding down the steps.

"Here comes Hurricane Hamish," said Charlie.

"Thank goodness," replied Fish. "We need him."

It started as applause and grew to the biggest roar and cheering and general mayhem from a crowd any of the players had ever known.

Hurricane was running on to the field of play, putting on his shirt as he went. People were banging drums, whistles were being blown – there was a cacophony of joyous celebration. The calypso cricketer had arrived. He sprinted out on to the field to replace Genus, his bare feet springing across the historic Sabina Park outfield. It was great to be there.

Hurricane ran up to Charlie and Fish.

"Where have you been?" Charlie said, raising an eyebrow at the boy. "And where did you get that bump on your head?"

Hurricane could only grin nervously.

"It's a long story, skipper."

"A good one?"

"Oh. It's a good one, OK," said Hurricane.

Charlie went over to Umpire Adams to confirm something. He came back and spoke to Hurricane.

"The rules say you've got to field for the same time you've been off. That's an hour – so we'll have to wait until after lunch to bowl you now. Let's hope Smith doesn't go too crazy in the meantime."

Smith, however, continued to bat relentlessly and magnificently – and was soon into the nineties. The West Indies were relieved when the interval came.

No one was surprised when the first thing Charlie Constantine did as the players took the field after lunch was to throw the ball to Hurricane.

"You owe me a few wickets," said Charlie, smiling now.

"I won't let you down. We haven't lost this one

yet. I'll give you those wickets," said Hurricane, "I promise."

He went to mark out his run. As he did so, he looked up to the place in the crowd where the girl had been — both for the trial and the Jamaica versus Trinidad game. He saw that the mystery girl was edging past people to take her seat. She turned and saw Hurricane looking up and raised her hand to him. Hurricane waved back.

He looked up at the scoreboard. 146 for 0. Smith 99 not out. Fish ambled over from mid-on. He put his arm around Hurricane's shoulder and said: "Be fast! You can do it! Be fast! Come on, Hurricane. It's more important than ever."

Hurricane charged in, his feet hardly seeming to touch the floor, he glided so gracefully into the wicket. His first ball was short outside the off stump. Smith flashed at it, hoping to steal the run he needed for his century, but the ball was through him too quickly and was in Alleyne's gloves before he even went through with the shot.

Andy Alleyne was standing a long way back, but he still took the ball way above his head. He tossed it to Charlie, who was at first slip, and whistled in appreciation at the sting in the palms of his hands.

"Now that *was* quick," he said.

Hurricane returned to his mark. He felt very loose, very strong. He charged in for the next delivery. It was full and straight and faster than the previous ball. It seemed to dart under Smith's helplessly flailing bat as if it had been pre-programmed to home in on the wicket. The ball was so fast that it simply snapped middle stump in two as it bowled Smith neck and crop.

The West Indies players ran to congratulate Hurricane. Smith trudged off, upset to have missed his century, but totally astonished by the speed of that delivery. He wished Hurricane had stayed away.

The crowd were dancing around. They had started a carnival. They knew that the West Indies were on their way.

FT tasted a bit of the swordfish steak and added some more butter to the pan. He was reading *The Caribbean Chronicle.*

Hurricane came over and looked over his shoulder.

"Now there's a mystery," he said. "Who's this bloke, the secret correspondent?"

"No one knows who the secret correspondent is," said FT. "Not even Harry Hack. No one's ever met the secret correspondent, Hurricane."

"I'd love to thank him," said Hurricane. "I wouldn't be playing at all if he hadn't sorted out that tape for the court, or sent that note to Charlie before this match. I wonder why he's so secretive?"

"No one knows that either," said FT.

He looked over at the boy and smiled. Hurricane was distracted but FT was going over the day's cricket in his mind.

"You want to know something Hurricane?" he said.

Hurricane looked up.

"What?"

"You were fast today. Properly fast," said FT with a smile.

Hurricane smiled back at him. It had been quite some day. Hurricane's arrival had set the crowd alight and had given a whole new impetus to the West Indies team. As well as picking up the vital wicket of Smith, Hurricane had also bowled Bingley and had Darcy caught at first slip by Charlie Constantine. He had bowled as fast and as accurately as he could remember – finishing with 3 for 37 off 20 overs. What was more, he had raised the spirits of the other bowlers. All of them had chipped in with wickets, as England collapsed to 289 all out, only Bertram and Wentworth managing any sort of a score after the opening pair had been dismissed. If the batsmen could do their stuff tomorrow, thought Hurricane, a win was back on the cards. The series might still be theirs.

Second Day
The batsmen did not do their stuff – indeed, by the time Hurricane walked out to the wicket later

on in the day, they had been reduced by England to 162 for 9.

It all started as badly as possible with ducks for both Constantine and Scorpio – West Indies were 0 for 2 at one stage. It was overcast throughout and the seam quartet of Willoughby, Wickham, Wentworth and Darcy moved the ball around all day – both in the air and off the wicket. There were some close lbw decisions which went England's way and two crazy run-outs, which could only be put down to the nerves of the occasion getting the better of some of the West Indies players. A few of the batsmen got a decent start, but none of them had gone on to make a big score.

Hurricane's march to the crease did not exactly fill anyone with confidence. His reputation preceded him, and on the one occasion he had batted so far in these Test matches he had been bowled first ball for a duck. Willoughby stood at the end of his run, licking his lips in anticipation. Hurricane always looked so awkward in his pads and gloves and helmet, and he had to wear boots for batting, which made him somehow unbalanced.

Fish Archibald was at the non-striker's end and walked down for a word.

"Shuffle across and just try and get something on it. We need every run we can muster. Do your best."

"I will," said Hurricane. "But I'm not very good at batting."

Fish smiled. As if he didn't know.

Willoughby knew this, too, and he delivered just what was required – a fast, straight yorker. Hurricane jabbed down on it too late and was bowled for yet another golden duck. The crowd let out a disappointed sigh and Hurricane hung his head in disappointment. West Indies all out for 162 – giving England a very healthy and potentially match-winning first innings lead of 127.

Hurricane came out at the back of the line, pleased to be taking the field with the rest of the team this time. Once again there was special applause for Fish in his hundredth Test and Hurricane took a few moments to marvel at the achievements of this great servant of cricket, who, like Charlie, had started playing for the West Indies nearly thirteen years ago, around the time FT found Hurricane wrapped up in the MCC towel.

The team gathered in a huddle in the way they had become accustomed to under Charlie Constantine. He got them thinking about the job in hand.

"Hurricane," he said. "I want you to take the first over. I'm going to set you straight at Smith. If we can get him out early we may have a chance of getting back into this game. An early breakthrough is vital."

Hurricane marked out his run and Fish came over from mid-off for his usual few words with him, encouraging Hurricane to really let it rip and give Smith a proper working over.

Hurricane's first ball was a no-ball, but it simply took off from just short of a length. Despite Andy Alleyne's desperate jump, it flew over the wicket-keeper's head and clattered into the sight-screen behind him for four byes. Smith stood back and twirled his bat, pretending to be unruffled, but thinking that he had never seen anyone as quick as this kid.

The next ball was legitimate, but just as fast. Smith flung his head back, flicked at it, got a thick edge and the ball flew all the way over the head of Sherwin Padmore at third man into the tenth row of the crowd for six. It had been so fast that Smith had merely helped it on its way.

Now Hurricane tried to bowl a slower one. Smith picked it, took two steps down the wicket and smashed it back over Hurricane's head for six more. The crowd was silenced. It was an incredibly aggressive start once again from Smith – fighting fire with fire.

Fish came over to Hurricane.

"Forget about the slower ones. Just be fast."

Hurricane nodded. More importantly, he searched once again for the familiar figure in the stand and managed to pick her out amongst the thousands of faces. The mystery girl was there.

"Be fast," he urged himself. "Come on. You can do it."

The next ball was the fastest Hurricane had ever bowled. It fired towards Smith's stomach. He jerked the bat up to protect himself but the ball smacked straight into the handle and the force flung the bat clean out of Smith's hands and on to his stumps.

Smith stood confused but Alleyne and the slips were shouting and Umpire Adams had his finger up. Smith was out hit wicket. The bat had simply been ripped from his hands by Hurricane's pace. England were 16 for 1.

Yet this was not the start of the batch of wickets the West Indies needed. For the rest of the day Martin and Ferrers dug in very effectively. Hurricane and Fish bowled well, but with no luck, and England finished the day on 66 for 1 – a lead of 193, and in a strong position to win the match.

Third Day
Everything came right for Hurricane on the third day. Only one man could cope with his blistering pace. George Knightley found his best form and batted quite beautifully for a glorious century.

The rest of the English batsmen found Hurricane too hot to handle. He got Martin early on for 25, then Ferrers for 30, Bingley for 2, Darcy for 8, Wentworth for 4 and Willoughby for 10. With Smith's wicket the day before this gave Hurricane

7 for 62 – his best Test figures to date.

He bowled tirelessly, accurately and with sustained hostility – it was a rare exhibition of the art of top-class pace bowling. Charlie asked him a couple of times if he wanted a breather, but Hurricane refused to come off.

Archibald, Amory and King also picked up a wicket each and England were all out, early on in the final session, for 272. The crowd simply rose to Hurricane as he led the team off. The boy had certainly come of age today – ten wickets in the match once again and he had carried the West Indies bowling attack.

The crowd was a knowledgeable one, though, and they were realists about the West Indies' chances. This bowling display was about as good as the West Indies could have hoped for, but it still left them with 400 to win – a very large score to make in the last innings of a Test match.

They started well enough, finishing the day on 60 for 0 – Charlie Constantine looking very comfortable on 19 and Radwick Scorpio having played some lovely shots to make 39. They needed 340 more to win – and the target still looked a fair way off.

Fourth Day
The West Indies started badly in the morning, losing Scorpio immediately and then Matthews cheaply to the bowling of Willoughby. They had

soon slumped to 67 for 2. The game had swung firmly England's way once again.

Yet, at the other end, Charlie Constantine was playing himself in to bat most of the day for one of the innings of his life. He played as well as any of the thousands of Jamaicans watching could ever remember him having played, scoring runs very quickly and stroking the England bowlers all around Sabina Park. Would anyone stay with him though? The West Indies lost James for 28 and Goldman for 17.

After lunch Constantine went to his century and the West Indies were now 189 for 4. Wicket-keeper Andy Alleyne joined him and batted very purposefully and with great aggression. The game was swinging back towards the West Indies until Wentworth found Alleyne's outside edge and keeper Churchill took the catch. 281 for 5. 119 still needed. The tension in the ground was unbearable.

Constantine had only Larry King and then the tail-enders for support now, so he continued to play his shots, trying to eat into the total as quickly as possible. King supported him well before being bowled by a sharp off-spinner from Bertram for 27.

322 for 6.

Padmore came and went quickly, caught at short leg off Wickham.

333 for 7.

There were 67 needed, but only three wickets

left – and one of those was Hurricane Hamish, yet to make a run in Test cricket.

The light was now coming in quickly – but by now Constantine and Amory were on top of the bowlers and putting together a very good partnership. The umpires offered the chance to come off for bad light but Charlie decided to bat on. The England team was getting edgy and Charlie felt on top of his game. The score edged upwards. 350. Then 360. Soon the West Indies were 370 for 7. Only 30 needed.

Darcy was juggling his bowlers as best he could, but his seamers were tired. 380 came up. A total hush enveloped the crowd as victory was coming within reach.

Charlie Constantine mopped his brow and called for a drink from the dressing-room. He had a chat with Roy Amory, telling him to keep going as he was – he was doing brilliantly.

Constantine hit Wickham for two boundaries through the off side and a two through mid-wicket.

390 for 7.

Darcy tossed the ball to Bertram. Constantine pushed him through mid-off for a quickly scampered single.

391 for 7.

Amory worked Bertram past point for 3.

394 for 7.

There were six needed. Charlie surveyed the

field, wondering whether to go for a big hit. The fifth ball of Bertram's over was slightly over-pitched. Constantine clipped it wide of mid-on for four.

398 for 7.

Only two more runs were needed. Bertram bowled again. The ball kept low and in the poor light Charlie could not get his bat on it in time and was hit on the pad. The whole England team shouted as one at Umpire Murray – Charlie had never heard a shout like it.

Owwwzzzaaaaaaaaaaaaaaaaaaattttttttttttttt!

Murray took some time over his decision, deciding that it had hit in line and was going on to take leg stump. The finger went up and the crowd groaned.

Then they rose as one to cheer Charlie off the ground after the most memorable of innings. He was out for 196, just short of a double-century, but a truly great innings in the context of the whole history of the game of cricket. No one could remember having seen anything quite like it.

398 for 8 – and it was even darker now, but only two overs were left in the day.

Fish Archibald came in and successfully played out a maiden from Darcy. It was far too accurate to try to steal a run. Now there was one over left. Amory had to decide whether to play for tomorrow or to try to steal the winning two runs.

Bertram bowled a perfect line and length to

Amory. He patted back the first five balls. The sixth span viciously and bounced, took Amory on the glove and bounced up to Smith at short leg, who caught it. A gasp went round the ground.

398 for 9.

West Indies were still two runs short and with only one wicket left. England captain Darcy claimed the extra time to try to finish the game off, but in the gloom the umpires offered Fish the light and he decided to come off.

That was it for the day.

West Indies number 11 Hurricane Hamish was left sitting in the dressing-room, shaking like a leaf, but not required until the morning.

Fifth Day

"At least nobody will turn up," said Hurricane hopefully at breakfast time.

FT looked up from his cooking.

"What do you mean?" he said quizzically.

"Well, the people aren't going to turn up just to see two runs or one wicket, are they?" said Hurricane.

FT shook his head and turned the kippers.

"I'm sorry Hurricane, but you've got to face it. The ground will be as packed as on the last four days. No one's ever seen a series like it and they are not going to miss the finale."

Hurricane put his head in his hands. He knew FT was right.

"Oh no," he muttered. "Don't they know I can't bat."

"Everybody knows you can't bat," said FT. "Everyone also hopes that somewhere, some day, you've got to get just one run – or even two. Perhaps that day will be today. You may not have to face any of the bowling anyway. Two to win, Fish on strike. It could be OK."

Hurricane groaned. Somehow he doubted it.

Hurricane walked to the ground and it reminded him of the day he had first played for Jamaica. People saw his lanky frame coming along the street and, before he knew it, he was surrounded by little kids, jumping up to touch him and wishing him luck. The message went down the streets in front of him on the way to the ground.

"Here he comes. Here comes Hurricane Hamish – the calypso cricketer!"

Old and young alike hung out of their windows and shouted out to him.

"Good luck, Hurricane."

"How about a run or two from you today."

"Calypso, Hurricane. Calypso."

Hurricane smiled and waved, but his nerves were jangling.

If it were possible, Sabina Park was even fuller than on the first four days. When Hurricane finally made it through the hordes of people up to the dressing-room, he looked out over the ground and took a minute to take in the scene. Even the Jamaican Blue Mountains behind the ground seemed to be straining towards the action – eager for their own view of this dramatic day of cricketing history. No one could have scripted it like this – the drama was so intense that it seemed like today the eyes of the whole of the world were on Sabina Park.

Hurricane was rather late. Fish Archibald was already sitting there with his pads on. He had a towel over his head, concentrating and getting his mind on the job in hand. The other players stood around in their West Indies blazers and team uniform, unable to do anything today, other than watch Fish and Hurricane decide if the series would belong to them or to England.

Hurricane got changed and padded up. A few of the players came to sit with him, talking to him, trying to build his confidence. He would never have minded being in a position to decide a series with the ball – but not with the bat! Fish was still under his towel, meditating.

England needed one wicket to win.

West Indies needed one run to tie, two to win.

The match and the whole series hung in the balance.

The umpires and the England fielders were out there and it was time for Fish and Hurricane to go. Fish had a grim look of determination on his face. Hurricane just looked worried. To try to change his luck, he left his boots in the dressing-room, deciding to risk it barefoot. He went gingerly out towards the field of play behind Fish.

As they were walking out Hurricane heard a voice to one side of him.

"Hurricane! Hurricane, over here!"

He looked at the mass of people packed around where the players came out.

"Hurricane!" came the voice again.

Hurricane scanned the faces and squashed in between them he made out the face of the mystery girl. Some people made a gap for her and she squeezed through to stand before him. He stopped, frozen in front of her.

"Who are you?" he said.

She looked very intensely at him and she spoke in a voice that was serious, yet full of belief.

"Don't worry about that now," she said. "Just remember. You don't know how to hold the bat. Last night I remembered a comment FT made to me that day at Black River. Try the other way. Just try the other way. Left-handed."

People were pushing to get a better view of Hurricane and the mystery girl disappeared back into the mass of people.

What did she mean?

There was a murmur from the crowd as Hurricane hesitated on the steps. All round the ground the crowd whispered to each other. What had Hurricane stopped for? Who had he been speaking to? Had he no boots on? Finally he came into view of the whole crowd as he started jogging on to the ground and caught up with Fish.

Inside the West Indian dressing-room Brian Lara turned to speak to Viv Richards.

Inside the England dressing-room Ian Botham turned to speak to Michael Atherton.

All round the ground people spoke in hushed tones to each other. They all said the same thing – uncertainty and anticipation in their words.

"Here comes Hurricane Hamish. Boots or no boots, I've never seen him make a run."

Fish was facing for the first over. Darcy took the captain's responsibility of bowling it. He had bowled accurately all series. If he could just keep Archibald at that end and prevent any runs, then Willoughby, their top fast bowler, could have a go at Hurricane Hamish in the next over. It was a risk, but it might just work.

Fish's plan was to play the first five balls of the over as positively as he could and to try to hit the runs. If not he would try to pinch a single off the last ball to keep the strike.

Darcy bowled the perfect defensive over. Each delivery was fired into the blockhole, he varied his pace, and it was all Fish could do to keep the six deliveries out – let alone hit the winning runs or even sneak a single off the last ball.

"Great bowling, captain," said Willoughby, taking the ball from him at the end of the over. The England players changed ends eagerly. Now they had a chance to bowl at Hurricane Hamish and none of them had ever seen him look like making a run.

Up in the dressing-room the West Indies players all groaned. Some could not even watch.

"That's it," someone said. "We've lost."

The crowd was quaking with nerves. Everyone was willing Hurricane to manage a good stroke. In their heart of hearts everyone knew that this was highly unlikely.

Fish sauntered down the wicket, pretending to be casual.

"Well this is it," said Fish. "It's now or never, Hurricane."

He looked at the kid. He liked him so much – but if only he could bat a bit.

"I've never even hit a ball in Test cricket before," said Hurricane.

"Isn't there something different you could try?" said Fish. "Anything?"

Hurricane remembered the mystery girl's words.

"Well. I've an idea," said Hurricane. "I've always been told I don't know how to hold a bat. So, how about the other way?"

"What?" said Fish. "You mean left-handed?"

"Why not?" said Hurricane. "Anything is worth a try. Otherwise we've lost."

Fish closed his eyes in prayer.

"Go on then," he said. "Try it."

Hurricane went back to the crease, took guard and settled into the stance of a left-hander.

Darcy switched his field round in response to this. John Willoughby stood at the end of his run, concentrating. To him, this seemed like desperation from Hurricane. Just one straight one – one straight delivery and the series should be theirs.

The crowd were so quiet it seemed unreal. Everybody had almost stopped breathing.

Hurricane felt the bat in the unusual position in his hand. It felt OK, he thought.

Willoughby charged in. He bowled a quick in-swinger on a full length, aiming for Hurricane's exposed toes. It curved in towards middle stump and Willoughby started to raise his arms as he saw it heading on target for victory.

Hurricane Hamish took a giant stride towards the ball and, lunging blindly, his eyes closed, he swung the bat towards it. He felt a contact with the ball and heard the noise of leather on willow.

For an instant everything stood still. Hurricane opened his eyes and saw the ball squeeze out on the leg side between square leg and mid-wicket. He looked up and Fish was haring down the wicket towards him.

"Run, Hurricane," he was screaming.

The whole crowd was screaming: "RUN, HURRICANE!"

Hurricane set off. With his bare feet, he flew over the turf. He reached the bowler's end in an instant and turned. Fish was already heading back towards him at full pelt.

"Run, Hurricane. There's two here."

The crowd was screaming and shouting.

"TWO, HURRICANE! RUN! RUN!"

Hurricane did not even look where the ball was. He ran like a madman down the wicket. Somewhere to his side he could hear the ball whistling in from the outfield. As he neared the wicket he dived, flinging himself full length and running his bat home before the ball thudded into Frank Churchill's gloves.

For a moment Hurricane lay outstretched on the turf. The world was suddenly full of noise – all he could hear was clapping and shouting and people calling his name. He could hear Fish somewhere.

"You did it, Hurricane. You did it."

Hurricane was carried off the ground by a group of supporters. He held his bat and the souvenir stump which someone had given him above his head. The whole ground was cheering and shouting and chanting his name and Hurricane grinned the biggest grin in the history of the world.

Fish, who was also being carried along in the air on a sea of people, called over to him.

"Hey, Hurricane!"

"What?" shouted Hurricane above the din.

"I always said you didn't know how to hold a bat!"

Hurricane was laughing. The crowd was chanting.

"Calypso! Calypso! Calypso!"

The series trophy was presented to Charlie Constantine and the Man of the Match award to Hurricane.

Hurricane stood with the two teams as he accepted the trophy from Man of the Match adjudicator Clive Lloyd. The West Indies team were all grinning and patting him on the back and, despite their disappointment, Mike Atherton, Fitzwilliam Darcy and the whole England squad were applauding him. Lara, Ambrose and Walsh were clapping and smiling, and the two Chairmen of selectors, Viv Richards and Ian Botham, stood together and marvelled at such a climax to one of the greatest ever Test series.

Hurricane looked out at the people crammed on to the outfield, shouting and waving up at him. Judge Herring was there pointing and shouting and Harry Hack was dancing and singing. Wesley was cheering and hugging FT. FT was laughing and was in tears. The mystery girl was smiling and waving. He tried to shout to her, but no one could hear anything for the noise.

Hurricane kissed the Man of the Match trophy

and raised it above his head, and Fish and Charlie hoisted him up on to their shoulders. He looked across the sea of smiling faces and waved in thanks to his adoring fans. He hoped that the secret correspondent, to whom he owed so much, was amongst them.

England

	1st Innings			2nd Innings		
S T L Smith		b Hamish	99	hit wicket	b Hamish	12
R Martin	lbw	b Padmore	60	c Alleyne	b Hamish	25
E S Ferrers	c Matthews	b King	15	lbw	b Hamish	30
C P Bingley		b Hamish	12	c Constantine	b Hamish	2
G Knightley	lbw	b Amory	4	c Alleyne	b King	111
F W Darcy*	c Constantine	b Hamish	0	c Archibald	b Hamish	8
E L Bertram		b Padmore	26	lbw	b Amory	20
F S Churchill+	lbw	b Amory	3		b Archibald	23
F R Wentworth		b King	30	c Alleyne	b Hamish	4
G D Wickham	c Alleyne	b Archibald	16		not out	17
J Willoughby		not out	6	lbw	b Hamish	10
Extras	(b6, lb6, nb6)		18	(lb3, nb5, w2)		10

Total   **(all out)** <u>**289**</u>   **(all out)** <u>**272**</u>

Fall of Wickets   1-146,2-164,3-181,4-193,5-197,   1-16,2-68,3-79,4-88,5-106,
6-221,7-235, 8-245,9-270,10-289   6-157,7-211,8-216,9-249,10-272

Bowling	O	M	R	W	O	M	R	W
F S Archibald	22.3	7	49	1	18	2	45	1
R P B Amory	12	0	57	2	17	0	47	1
S T Padmore	13	0	45	2	9	0	27	0
L V A King	25	7	89	2	28	6	88	1
H Hamish	20	9	37	3	30.5	10	62	7

West Indies

	1st Innings			2nd Innings		
C Constantine*	lbw	b Wickham	0	lbw	b Bertram	196
R Z Scorpio	lbw	b Wentworth	0	c Ferrers	b Willoughby	39
R P Matthews		b Darcy	46	c Churchill	b Willoughby	4
J J James	lbw	b Bertram	18	c Darcy	b Wentworth	28
B Goldman	c Martin	b Willoughby	15	lbw	b Darcy	17
A C Alleyne+		run out	22	c Churchill	b Wentworth	50
L V A King	lbw	b Darcy	31		b Bertram	27
S T Padmore		run out	9	c Knightley	b Wickham	3
R P B Amory	c Willoughby	b Wickham	9	c Smith	b Bertram	24
F S Archibald		not out	7		not out	0
H Hamish		b Willoughby	0		not out	2
Extras	(b2, lb3)		5	(b1, lb3, nb4, w2)		10

Total   **(all out)** <u>**162**</u>   **(for 9 wickets)** <u>**400**</u>

Fall of Wickets   1-0,2-0,3-43,4-81,5-100,   1-60,2-67,3-122,4-154,5-281,
6-128,7-139,8-150,9-162,10-162   6-322,7-333,8-398,9-398

Bowling	O	M	R	W	O	M	R	W
J Willoughby	12.2	2	40	2	31.1	4	98	2
G D Wickham	14	1	49	2	21	6	84	1
F R Wentworth	10	0	21	1	18	2	73	2
F W Darcy	10	3	33	2	17	3	65	1
E L Bertram	4	1	14	1	27	1	76	3

Man of the Match: H Hamish (West Indies)
West Indies won by 1 wicket

Epilogue

The Secret Correspondent

Treasure Beach, Jamaica

The season had finished and the commotion surrounding the most exciting Test series that the Caribbean had ever seen was gradually dying down. Hurricane was pleased to have a break from all the attention he had been getting. After all, he was a solitary person, not used to the glare of publicity. He was pleased, at least for a while, to be back to the normality of his life at Treasure Beach with FT.

A lot had happened in the days after the Test. The secret correspondent had written an article exposing Rich Vermin and all of the plots which had taken place throughout the series. The police had found Rich Vermin in the barn, crying like a baby. He was arrested and charged with corruption and kidnapping. Rough Tungsten had disappeared. It seemed that he had followed Otis Campbell into hiding. The police were looking for them both.

Hurricane was just pleased to have some peace

again, and was able to be where he loved to be most. He was able to walk the wide, dark sandy beach alone; he was able to swim in the beautiful water and to body-surf the waves; he was able to sail the boat out and to fish the Pedro Banks; and he was able to take dinner home to FT and affectionately watch the old man make a stunning banquet of the day's catch. He was thinking about the mystery girl, though. All the time.

One day Hurricane was wandering down the beach alone, with the old MCC towel Judge Herring had given him tucked under his arm. This was a day much like any other. It was hot and the sky was clear, with not even a wisp of cloud. The tide was going out as he walked the shore, and with each step he dug his toes into the soft, wet, black sand beneath his feet. He was miles away, alone with his thoughts, reliving the fears and triumphs of those recent times, wallowing especially in his memories of the games in Antigua, Barbados and Jamaica and the wonderful three-two victory over the English.

His mind turned also to his next challenge. The West Indies were off to England for the one-day competition – the Cricket World Cup. He hoped to goodness the selectors would pick him. He could not wait to get over there and see all the grounds he had read about and seen on TV. FT would come, too, and he could show him the old weather vane on top of the Grandstand at Lord's.

He walked his usual way, all the way along the sand towards the familiar and reassuring sight of the small fishing boat tucked away against the rocks at the end of the beach. Wesley Clarke had arranged for it to be returned by the police from Black River Bay, where the villains had dumped it after they kidnapped Hurricane.

The sun caught the side of the boat and, as he approached it, Hurricane was satisfied to see that the red hull was gleaming. He neared the boat and could make out the words *The Hurricane* painted in black at the bow. It was good to have it back.

His eyes, though, were drawn to something else – to a white shape on the beach. Close to the boat he could make out a towel – a gleaming white towel which had been laid out flat on the black sand. Hurricane approached it cautiously, squatted down on his haunches next to it, and stared at it quizzically. Some gold lettering in the corner of the towel caught his eye. There were three beautifully embroidered letters – MCC. On top of the towel was a pad and a pencil.

This was uncanny. Whose towel was it and what was it doing here? Who was the writer? He laid his own towel beside it – the two making a pair on the black sand.

Hurricane was vaguely conscious of being watched, but he could not think by whom or from where. He looked out across the water and he saw a shape bobbing in the water, the head of someone swimming, quite far out to sea. The person raised an arm and waved to him. He waved back – to whom he did not know yet. Presumably it was the owner of the towel – and of the pad and pencil.

The swimmer came in closer and gradually he made out the face of a girl – that familiar face of the mystery girl who had seemed almost to lay the path for the events of the last few months. She had made it all possible, after all. As she swam closer, he could clearly see her long black hair. Here she was again – the mystery girl who turned up everywhere, but who had always been so hard to find.

The mystery girl swam to the shore and walked out of the water.

She was very beautiful. He suddenly felt very awkward and embarrassed. She took up her towel and wrapped it around her. She smiled to him – a bright, dazzling, lovely smile, unlike any he had ever seen before.

"I never expected to see you again," he said. "Never to actually speak to you."

"I guessed I might see you here," she said.

He wanted to talk. There was so much he had to tell her, but he felt suddenly tongue-tied and all the conversations he had had with her in his mind seemed suddenly far away. He was too embarrassed to tell her that every time he saw her he had started to bowl well, that she had been like a force which had got him through the games, that he thought she was very beautiful, that...

She broke the silence.

"Well played," she said. "I've never had the chance to say that to you face to face."

Hurricane stared at his feet. Words seemed hopeless, too inadequate to say how he felt.

He forced himself to speak.

"Thanks for saving me from Rich Vermin and getting me to the Test. I don't know how to thank you."

She laughed.

"You did thank me. You made a run – two runs, at last. And you bowled so well, all along."

"I feel I owe you for that, too," he said. "You don't know it, but you sort of helped me to bowl well – and to bowl fast. Just by being there. Whenever I saw you. If it hadn't been for you and the secret correspondent none of this would ever have happened."

She smiled at him. She knew what he meant, but the time had come to tell him the whole story. She had not been just another kid in the crowd, after all.

"You've got more to thank me for than you know," she said.

Hurricane looked up from the sand into her dark, dark eyes.

"Why?" he asked.

"Didn't you realize, Hurricane?" she said. "I AM the secret correspondent."

The world seemed to go silent and there was only the sound of the swell of the sea.

Hurricane's brain started to take it all in. Of course. It all made sense.

"What, you?" he said. "You were the one who wrote all those things helping me! You were the one who sent that tape with Harry Hack to the courthouse! You were the one who sent Charlie the note to ask him to give me time to get to the game! And here you are with the MCC towel which Harry Hack said he'd give to the secret correspondent! No wonder the secret correspondent seemed to know when you'd be at the cricket!"

"Yes," she said. "It was me all along."

Everything was fitting into place at last.

"But your voice," said Hurricane. "Why didn't Harry Hack suspect something?"

"I always disguised it," she admitted. "I got used to doing that whenever I spoke to Harry Hack. I couldn't have everyone knowing the secret correspondent was a girl. They'd make me go to school. I'd have lost my job."

Hurricane smiled.

"That's why you didn't want me to get to know you, even when you'd driven me to Sabina Park in the van. You needed it all to stay a secret."

"Exactly," said the mystery girl. "A secret you and I now share. And don't ever tell anyone I drove a van down from the Blue Mountains. I still don't know how I got us to the match."

Hurricane laughed.

"So it was you writing all those articles to help me and the team during the series?" asked Hurricane.

"Yes. That's why no one at the paper knows me. They just contact me on the secret number. I send the articles in, and they print them."

"The towel..." said Hurricane.

"That's it – that's where I got this towel. Harry sent it to me."

Hurricane shook his head. This was amazing, but wonderful.

"You look too young to work on a newspaper," he said. "You're only my age."

She smiled at him and she had a teasing glint in her eye.

"So I'm too young to be a writer, am I, but you are old enough to play cricket for the West Indies? You should be in school – like old Judge Herring said."

Hurricane laughed.

"Fair enough," he said. "Maybe we're both old enough."

"Who says kids can't change the world?" she replied mischievously.

Then Hurricane chuckled out loud.

"As old FT says, if you're good enough, you're old enough," he said.

She laughed with him and that made him laugh more and soon they were both laughing like crazy together.

"I hope you can make it over to England for the Cricket World Cup if I'm picked," Hurricane said.

"I'll try," she said, still laughing. "I think you'll be there."

The waves lapped the shore.

"Since I'm quoting him, would you like to come and see FT?" Hurricane asked, picking up his towel. "He's a big fan of your writing."

The secret correspondent smiled.

"I would love to meet him," she said. "But that will have to be our secret."

"OK," said Hurricane. "But can you tell me your name?"

She smiled.

"Cordelia."

The two of them walked side by side down Treasure Beach. It was a beautiful day and the sun was at its highest in the sky. The rays played on the surface of the Caribbean Sea and made beautiful patterns with the green and blue shades of the water.

Appendix: Test Series Averages

Batting	M	I	NO	Runs	HS	Ave
S T L Smith	5	9	0	610	214	67.78
R Martin	5	9	0	396	98	44.00
G Knightley	4	7	0	285	111	40.71
W T Collins	1	2	0	70	44	35.00
H P A Tilney	1	2	0	61	49	30.50
F W Darcy	5	9	0	262	65	29.11
G D Wickham	5	9	6	83	21*	27.67
C P Bingley	5	9	0	225	56	25.00
E S Ferrers	4	7	0	110	36	15.71
E L Bertram	5	9	0	116	26	12.89
W A Eliot	1	2	0	25	17	12.50
F R Wentworth	4	7	0	86	30	12.29
J Willoughby	5	9	4	58	11	11.60
H P Crawford	1	2	0	22	22	11.00
F S Churchill	4	7	0	75	23	10.71

Bowling	O	M	R	W	Ave
J Willoughby	174.4	31	540	23	23.48
E L Bertram	149	33	422	15	28.13
H P A Tilney	27	12	30	1	30.00
F W Darcy	128	34	351	11	31.91
G D Wickham	158	33	503	15	33.53
F R Wentworth	102	10	368	10	36.80

Catches

11 – Churchill; 4 – Darcy; 3 – Knightley, Smith, Willoughby; 2 – Crawford, Ferrers, Martin; 1 – Bertram, Collins, Eliot, Tilney, Wentworth

West Indies

Batting	M	I	NO	Runs	HS	Ave
C Constantine	5	10	3	565	204*	80.71
R Z Scorpio	2	4	1	136	68	45.33
A C Alleyne	5	9	3	254	80	42.33
R P Matthews	5	9	0	358	113	39.78
L V A King	5	8	1	198	67*	28.29
B Goldman	5	9	0	250	104	27.78
J J James	5	9	0	197	50	21.89
O K Campbell	3	6	0	95	39	15.83
F S Archibald	5	7	2	45	18	9.00
S T Padmore	4	7	2	41	18*	8.20
R P B Amory	5	7	0	39	24	5.57
F R Genus	3	5	1	4	4	1.00
H Hamish	3	3	1	2	2*	1.00

Bowling	O	M	R	W	Ave
H Hamish	137.5	31	379	29	13.07
F S Archibald	197.3	39	537	22	24.41
F R Genus	82.3	21	205	7	29.29
L V A King	227	61	620	16	38.75
R P B Amory	153.5	21	489	10	48.90
S T Padmore	85	5	300	4	75.00
R Z Scorpio	2	1	2	0	–

Catches

17 – Alleyne (+ 1 stumping); 6 – Constantine; 4 – Matthews; 3 – Archibald, Genus;
2 – Amory, Campbell, James, King, Padmore; 1 – Goldman, Scorpio

---

Key: *Batting: Matches, Innings, Not Outs, Runs, Highest Score, Average*
Bowling: Overs, Maidens, Runs, Wickets, Average

Don't miss Hurricane's next adventure:

HURRICANE
HAMISH THE CRICKET
WORLD CUP

Hurricane Hamish is back – and this time he's in England, determined to help the West Indies win the Cricket World Cup. But he soon finds that English grounds aren't what he's used to. They're so *cold* and *wet* and *slippery*. It's hard enough to stand up, let alone bowl fast. Hurricane came to England a hero, but he could be about to make a fool of himself – in front of the whole world...